Crimson

A Novel

A. L. Singer

ISBN: 978-0-9851848-4-1

This is a work of fiction. All of the characters, names, incidents, organizations, events, and dialogue in this novel are either the products of the author's imagination or are used fictitiously.

Cover art by Tham Nguyen Design.

Acknowledgments

To my husband and siblings who have been amazing through this whole experience, thank you for your continuous support and encouragement.

To my prereaders—Natalie, Gina, Kim, Laura, and Adam—your opinions and feedback have been a joy and very entertaining.

To my aunt, godmother, and stepmother, I love you equally.

To the two I have loved and lost—this has been a bittersweet journey without you.

To my editor, Lisa Drucker, thank you for all your help, hard work, and encouragement.

Chapter 1

I sighed and went to my bedroom, roughly flicking on my bedroom light and leaving the door open behind me. Once alone in my room, I happily slipped out of my shoes and dress. I discarded the rest of my garments and headed to the bathroom for a bath. I filled the tub with extra-hot water so I could lengthen the duration of my soak. Adding the salts Sorin had given me, I eased myself into the water. My skin turned pink from the water's temperature, but I didn't mind. I lay my head back and closed my eyes; it was semidark, with only the bedroom light spilling into the bathroom.

My thoughts automatically shifted to Sorin. Where had he gone and where would he stay till the sun came up? I thought of Anya, convincing myself to trust that she really had left the area. Despite being surrounded by hot water, goose bumps spread over my arms. I brushed my cheek with my fingertips, still baffled that I could feel Sorin's physical pain. And that was with only a few drops of my blood within him. What horrible pain he must have experienced, mentally and physically, as he felt my mother slowly die. Tears welled up, and I allowed them to fall. I felt suddenly aware of what this past week must have been like for him. I imagined it was the same hell I was experiencing, maybe even twice as bad. My heart ached for Sorin, for his mirrored pain, and for his presence. For a moment I wanted to call out to him, in the hope he was still in the house.

Recalling some of my favorite memories with my parents, my tears increased. The water eventually cooled, and I drained it. After stepping out of the tub, I dried off and wrapped a towel around myself. I stepped into the bedroom and stopped to look at the empty bed. For days now, I had fallen asleep lying next to Sorin and woken up beside him. I sighed, irritated at my conflicting emotions. I crossed to the light switch and pushed it down. I took a step to the doorway, no longer able to resist calling out for him. A part of me wanted to be alone. I still had a lot to contemplate. But a deeper part needed his presence.

"Sorin?" I said, raising my voice to be sure he would hear me. My heart started to quicken, and I held my breath. After no movement or sounds came from downstairs, I tugged at the towel around me, letting it fall to the floor. I had turned the air conditioning down drastically while hanging the curtains, in an effort to make the temperature more comfortable for Sorin. Having done so, I was now overly warm, but I remained optimistic that I would adjust after a few days. I crawled into bed and pulled the light sheet over myself.

So many thoughts still filled my head. I was beginning to wonder what a life with Sorin would be like. I buried my head deeper into my pillow. I knew the thought of him leaving for good distressed me. But the option of living multiple lifetimes still held little appeal for me. I closed my eyes and touched where he had left the small bruises, envisioning Sorin cradling my arm and briefly tasting me. Possibly he'd caused a permanent bond between us, but the thought did not repulse me. I only wanted a little more time to decide if it was what I truly desired. To feel there was something I could control the outcome of. He had looked so handsome standing at the bottom of the stairs and waiting for me before dinner. I was gradually feeling more for Sorin as each day passed, and it was vastly unexpected. It was difficult to fall asleep without him next to me.

Sleep eventually took me, and the dark engulfed my vision. I dreamed of painting and focusing on the brushstrokes of the tree I was beginning. My phone rang in my dream, and I stared at it, afraid to answer. It rang again, jolting me awake. I did not recognize the number but answered it anyway.

"Hello?" I said, still groggy.

"Yes, hello … this is James Szurpicki. … I called a few days ago. I was interested in acquiring your services if possible. Sorry to have woken you." He fumbled over his words.

I looked at the alarm clock sitting on my dresser. It was past noon. He was probably surprised I had been asleep so late in the day. I cleared my throat and sat up. "No … no … don't apologize, Mr. Szurpicki. I did get your message. I am so sorry for not returning your call. I have been really busy." I hoped my voice sounded sincere and wished he would take the hint I wasn't interested.

"No, no … I understand," he quickly responded. His voice told me he somehow knew everything. A downside to living in a small town: there were few secrets. He knew about my parents. I was quiet, not sure what to say. During my silence, he continued. "I mean … I have seen your artwork … and I'm sure you are busy with other clients." He sounded apologetic, trying to cover up any slip he had just made.

My patience was wearing thin. I didn't want to accept the job, but I promised myself I would take it one day at a time. Maybe painting again would be a step in the right direction. Another distraction besides Sorin. A way to feel like myself again. "I am free today if you would like to discuss exactly what you are looking for and what my fee would be." I was already awake; I felt indifferent about meeting him, but knew I would likely take the job offer.

Mr. Szurpicki gave me the new pizzeria's address. I remembered a building on the edge of town that had been empty for years, but I scribbled down the address just in case I was wrong. He said they were setting up tables and chairs, so he would be in for the next few hours.

I dressed and went downstairs, heading toward the kitchen. On the way, I gathered a few of the curtains to let some sunlight in. This was the first day in a long time that I felt really hungry. I pushed some buttons on the oven to start heating it. Pulling open the refrigerator door, a bittersweet feeling came over me as I looked at the black bag in front of me. I tried to remember what Sorin had said was in the bag. Something parmesan; it had sounded good at that time. I took out the bag and placed it on the counter. I opened the first container and looked over its contents. Traditional spaghetti in marinara sauce. Then a penne pasta in pesto sauce. Next was the linguine with clam sauce. The last box held what I had been searching for: eggplant parmesan. Dumping the whole serving into a pan, I placed it in the oven. I packed away the rest of the food and returned the bag to the fridge. While the food heated, I went back up to my room, brushed my hair, and put on a little makeup.

After a while the aroma of eggplant parmesan made its way upstairs. My stomach growled, and I rushed back down to the kitchen. I ate the meal straight from the pan. With no one around to judge, I didn't feel embarrassed about my etiquette. I shut off the oven and rinsed out the pan. Grabbing my keys and sunglasses, I shoved the paper that held the address into my pocket. Passing the stool Sorin always sat on when in the kitchen with me, I missed him even more. I hurried out of the kitchen and left the house.

The quickest way to the pizzeria included the road where my mother's coffee shop was located. It called out to me as I drove past. I considered stopping in, but all the tables outside were full of customers enjoying the summer weather. *Maybe on the way home,* I told myself. Days had passed without Jennifer calling to check up on me again. I should at least stop to visit.

I found the pizzeria easily. There was a large truck in front of it, and multiple men were unloading furniture. I made my way inside, excusing myself as I went past the men working.

A man came out and moved around the corner of the counter. He gave me big smile. "Mia?" he asked, just as a confirmation.

"Mr. Szurpicki?" I said, extending my hand.

He continued to smile as he shook my hand. "Oh ... call me James, please." He was much taller than I, and he had short dark-brown hair and brown eyes. He struck me as a man who had played football all through his high school years. Broad shoulders and a rather thick neck. "Excuse the mess; we are a little behind schedule," he said, flustered.

Someone behind the bar dropped a glass and swore as it shattered.

James rolled his eyes. "Same dance ... different day," he mumbled. His face was flushed, and I noticed a few beads of sweat on his brow. He ushered me past the counter.

We spent about an hour walking around the building, and he described where the tables would be and what the décor would be like. Every few minutes or so, employees would interrupt to ask for further instructions on their current projects. Eventually, we got through our discussion. We agreed on the size and content of the paintings. After we settled on a deadline, he wrote out a check for the first half of my fee. I always used that for the supplies I needed. Upon delivery of the paintings, I would collect the other half. We said our good-byes, and I left, already mentally making a list of the supplies I would need.

But all I wanted to do was go back home and crawl into bed. Feeling tired, I wondered how many hours I had actually slept. Sorin wasn't in my bed or waiting for me, so there was no reason to hurry home. Knowing if I didn't run to the next town over for supplies now, I would have to go tomorrow, I headed in that direction. I was already out of the house; why not push myself a little further? I picked up the supplies I needed: a few new paintbrushes and every large canvas they had in stock. Years before, I had made a deal with the owner that I would only purchase my supplies from his store. In exchange, I received a small discount, and the store would deliver anything I could not transport myself. I set up a delivery for a few hours later.

Passing the coffee shop again on the way home, I noticed that only a young couple sat outside. I pulled into a parking spot and shut off the car. I sat and lay my head back against the seat, debating if I should put off visiting the mama bears one more day. I closed my eyes, knowing it had to be done. A knock on my window made me jump, and my eyes shot open. Jennifer stood there, looking into my window and mouthing, "Sorry." I took the keys from the ignition, slowly opening the door as she stepped back.

Jennifer forced a smile. "Hello there, stranger." She sounded hurt that I hadn't been in touch. This was expected and came as no surprise to me. I shut my car door and knew a hug was only moments away. So I stepped to her side and hugged her.

"I'm sorry I have not called … really." I swallowed hard, struggling with the knot in my throat.

"We were starting to worry about you. I was actually going to come by tonight after I closed up." Her voice cracked a little, and she let go of me only to lead me inside. I reluctantly followed. "The girls will be so happy you came by. I thought it was your car that drove by around lunchtime." She looked at me inquisitively.

"I was on my way to an appointment," I told her. "I'm going to do some paintings for the new pizzeria on the edge of town." I shrugged. "Maybe it is time to join the world again." My tone was flat.

Jennifer stopped me just before opening the door next to us. "It's normal that you needed some time alone, Mia. The girls and I just reopened the shop yesterday. We all needed some time." She weakly smiled, and when I remained silent because I couldn't decide what to say, she opened the door for us. "Let's go say hi," she said, nodding for me to go first.

I stepped past her and walked into the shop. Gina and Natalie came out from behind the counter. I had only met Natalie a few times before. She was a close friend of the twins and had just moved back to town. She had only started working in the shop two weeks earlier.

Gina stretched her arms out to greet me. "Hello, mama bear." I said, trying to smile. She hugged me, and Jennifer quickly moved to her sister's side.

All three women stood before me, wearing their black pants and crisp white shirts. They all had their hair pulled back, and Gina's black apron was speckled in flour. My eyes drifted to the flour in Gina's dark-caramel hair, and I brushed it away. "Are you creating something in the kitchen today?" I attempted to head off any deep conversation.

Gina brushed at her apron. "Oh … yeah, I am trying out a new cookie recipe. It's Hungarian and has a fruit filling. You would like it, Mia. Come by tomorrow, and I will have some with pineapple in them for you." Her voice held a subtle plea.

I smiled and nodded. "I will try to come by."

We all stood for a minute in an uneasy silence. Jennifer finally stepped forward and turned me to face the wall that usually held my paintings. "You didn't notice, did you?" She gently squeezed my elbow. "We sold the last two yesterday."

I looked around at the other walls, which held a variety of local artists' paintings. Ordinarily, I would have felt proud, but now I wondered about the timing. I smiled and tried to look pleased. "I was just telling Jennifer I accepted a job to do all the artwork at the local pizzeria. It shouldn't take me long. Maybe after that I will do a new series for the wall."

The set of paintings that I had done last were of gardens. It had been my least favorite of all the many series I had done over the years. But I usually asked the mama bears what they suggested. So, just like every other time when the last painting sold, I asked for ideas. "What do you mama bears think I should paint next?" I stared at the empty wall, one hand on my hip. Half of the money from my artwork went to the coffee shop. It was my contribution to my mother's business. Kayla worked weekends for little pay to help out.

Gina spoke up first. "Maybe some pretty sunsets?"

Jenny nudged her. "She's already done that." Jenny looked at the wall, her expression blank.

I turned to Natalie. She had an odd look and was chewing on the inside of her cheek. She was plump and a few inches shorter than the twins. Her skin had tanned since the last time I saw her, and I noticed freckles that weren't there before. She was fighting speaking up. "I think it would be nice to hear what your newest partner has to suggest," I said.

Natalie's eyes widened, and she looked a little nervous to be put on the spot. "Well, Jennifer and Gina were telling me about some of your past artwork." She listed a few of the pieces I'd done. "Flowers, fruit, lighthouses ..." I nodded as she mentioned each one. "I was thinking of something a little different." She stopped and began to fidget.

"Go on," I said, happy to know it wouldn't be something cliché, given the way she was acting. "Well, I know it is kind of a conservative town ... but maybe some figures." She paused, and I gave her an intrigued look to encourage her to explain further. "I was reading my horoscope the other day, and I thought each astrological sign could be turned into a beautiful figure. Male or female depending on your preference or the sign," she finished.

It actually sounded exciting; it was so different from all the fruit and flowers I usually did. It awakened my desire to paint—not because I had to, but because I wanted to. "How do you feel about nudity, if I did it tastefully?" I asked. My mother would have said to go with whatever inspiration I was feeling. But the sisters were always a little less adventurous than my mother when it came to art.

Mixed opinions greeted my question, but Natalie beamed, happy I was interested in her suggestion. The sisters looked at one another, clearly uncomfortable at the thought. Jennifer lightly winced. "We need to remember that families come here too, Mia. We don't want to offend any customers." She said it as gently as she could.

I understood that the dynamics had changed a little now that my mother, their friend, was gone. I had no qualms about a compromise. "Why don't I paint the series, and then you can hang up the ones you feel comfortable with."

All three smiled, and then a group of young girls entered the shop.

"It will be a few weeks before I even start them." I waved good-bye as I excused myself.

They returned to their places behind the counter and started helping the group of girls with their orders. Natalie slipped back into the kitchen, offering one last smile as I looked back.

I walked out, ready to return to the solitude of my house.

Chapter 2

As I stepped across the threshold, I wondered if all this was too much to take on. I shut the door behind me and leaned against it. I was enjoying the silence of my empty house when I realized water was running. Pushing myself away from the door, I walked softly to the bottom of the staircase, listening more intently. The sound of the water was coming from downstairs, and it was the shower. I slipped off my shoes and padded toward the guest room. The kitchen was poorly lit, as the foyer curtains were the only ones I had opened earlier. Careful not to bump into anything, I stepped as gently as I could all the way to the guest room door. The water shut off just as I reached the guest room.

My heart leaped; it had to be Sorin. I wondered how he had been able to return on such a sunny day; plus I hadn't seen his SUV in the driveway. Still, I knew it couldn't be anyone else. I considered walking in on him and felt butterflies stir inside me. On more than one occasion, I had imagined the details of the body concealed by his clothes. He had always been respectful of my privacy when I dressed or undressed. It would only be proper for me to do the same. A part of me said I should knock. But the possibility of seeing him naked and vulnerable made my pulse increase. I slowly pressed the door open, and what I saw was more than I expected.

The room was dark; a small amount of light filtered in from the open bathroom door. Sorin stood frozen in the doorway of the bathroom, holding a towel closed around his hips. Every muscle in his body tensed at the sight of me. Any anger or frustration I still felt about the previous night out and the confessions that had resulted from it now melted away instantly. My body screamed to run to him, to touch his exposed skin. All was truly forgiven if this was what Sorin had felt during his first moments alone with me. I resisted touching him but could not stop myself from looking over every inch of his body. He had very little hair on his toned chest. His stomach was flat and his arms were muscular. My eyes drifted past the towel at his waist, disappointed by how much it covered. It fell just above his knees, so I was able to see his calves. They were just as toned as the rest of his body. Sorin was actually thinner than I had imagined but much more muscular.

He coughed lightly, and my cheeks warmed, but only slightly. I looked up from his legs. Surprise had left his face, which now only expressed what seemed to be insecurity. I had experienced feeling self-conscious myself lately. But seeing his body, he had nothing to be embarrassed about.

After a few seconds, I said the first thing that popped into my head. "I'm sorry ... I thought there was intruder. ... I mean, I didn't see your SUV in the driveway, so ..." I let my voice trail off. I hadn't seen his SUV in the driveway, but the rest was a blatant lie. We both knew it.

His face showed just how much he believed my excuse for walking in on him. "Mia, have I not been a gentleman ever since I arrived? I have certainly tried my best."

I closed the door behind me and rested against it. I didn't want Sorin to leave, though I thoroughly understood I couldn't stop him if he tried. My heart pounded, and I didn't want this moment to end. I felt excited, even giddy—all the negative emotions I had been feeling left me momentarily. "You don't have to be a gentleman anymore," I said, stunned by my own assertiveness. My eyes drifted over his body again, as

I began to wonder why my intentions were not being reciprocated. I felt there was a definite attraction between us. We argued with, hurt, and frustrated one another, but all that seemed a distant memory. I felt myself fight a grin. "Sorin, a gentleman doesn't sleep in a woman's bed without asking. Or ... take from her without permission." My fingers instinctively touched my arm where he had bitten me. I looked up at his face to see frown lines were present. I had hurt his feelings without intending to. "I'm not upset anymore ... really," I added quickly, wanting to put him at ease. He still hadn't moved from the doorway. He looked so guarded. I knew if anything was going to happen, I would have to initiate. "Sorin, don't you find me ... attractive?" I whispered, the question leaving my lips easily.

Finally his body relaxed. His eyes trailed down my body, and I took it as an invitation, stepping toward him. Sorin's eyes quickly met mine, and his free hand shot out, warning me to stop. His body tensed up again, and his eyes cleared of any thoughts he had just entertained. "Mia ... it is much more complicated than that." His voice was firm.

I wanted to press myself against him and feel his arms around me. I couldn't decide if he was trying to be honorable or if there was really more to it. Either way, I was beginning to feel that rejection was just moments away. Still, I didn't want to back down. "It can be simple, Sorin." I slowly took another step his direction, hesitantly because I didn't know how he would respond. "We don't have to overthink this." Another step. "I want you ... I know what I am doing. You won't be taking advantage of me." No longer hesitant, I practically threw myself at him, grabbing the bottom of my shirt and starting to pull it up. I wondered if a little exposed flesh would make Sorin surrender to the moment. Our eyes locked, but my shirt had only risen a few inches when the bathroom light went out.

I shoved my shirt back down and didn't bother to hold back the groan expressing the complete frustration that filled me. I stomped my foot and cautiously backed to the door behind me. I heard Sorin moving in the dark and knew he would be dressed before I could find the light switch.

His voice finally sounded in the darkness. "I am sorry, Mia. ... Tru—"

I cut him off. "You are not sorry!" I shot back, infuriated. "You know what I am saying is true." I had heard a touch of disappointment in his voice. He was telling the truth; I had no bitter taste in my mouth, which only confused me further. "Fine!" I said through gritted teeth. "You meant it when you said you're sorry."

Finding the switch to the overhead light, I flipped it on. He was completely dressed, pulling a sweater over his head. I opened my mouth to continue yelling at him, needing some form of release.

Sorin stopped moving, and his expression changed. He looked at me with pure relief. "You have company, Mia." He reached down to retrieve a pair of socks. I crossed my arms, trying to stand my ground. The doorbell chimed, and I let out a sound of disgust at the timing.

I opened the guest room door and shot a look back at him. All the way to the front door, I kept talking, telling Sorin what I thought about the situation and that we were not done talking. I flung the front door open, and a teenage boy from the art supply store stood in the doorway. His eyes widened at my sudden presence. He had never made a delivery for me before. "Yes?" I said, annoyed.

He looked down at a slip of paper in his hand and then at the number on the mailbox. He hardly looked old enough to drive. "I—I think I have a delivery for you. Fifteen canvases?" He was unsure.

I opened the door completely and ushered him inside. "You're early … just put them at the bottom of the stairs, please," I said over my shoulder as I headed to the kitchen to retrieve some money to tip him. While locating a twenty-dollar bill, I heard him make multiple trips with the canvases.

We both stood and counted them to make sure all fifteen were there. I thanked him, walked him to the door, and handed him the cash.

Before going back to the kitchen, I closed the few curtains that were open. At the last one, I heard a stool in the kitchen slide over the floor. I turned the kitchen lights on as I entered the room. Sorin was sitting in his stool, and I walked past him to start a kettle of water for tea.

"I can move the canvases up to the attic for you, Mia," he offered, trying to smooth things over.

I shrugged in response, not willing to let go of my irritation so easily. Instead of the blur I was anticipating, he slowly left the kitchen. I heard him make a few trips up and down the stairs. My father had always helped me in the past when the canvases were as large as I was. I'd considered asking the delivery boy for help, but I'd really just wanted him gone so I could talk to Sorin.

The kettle screamed as he reentered the kitchen. I shut off the burner on the stovetop and placed a teacup on the island's marble top. He sat back down as I chose which flavored tea I wanted.

"Why?" I finally said, my voice raised as I turned to face him. Sorin looked at me with a touch of annoyance. "Why are you … refusing something … I think we both want?" I pressed.

His eyes fell from mine to the teacup that sat on the counter an arm's length away. In a fluid movement, he picked it up. I crossed my arms, still waiting for an answer. His eyes met mine for a moment, and then he raised the teacup in the air between us. In an instant, it shattered in his hand. I jumped slightly at the unexpected sound. I tightened my jaw and felt my fingers dig into my arms. He slowly lowered his fist to the counter in front of him, turning his hand over so all the pieces clattered noisily as they fell onto the marble.

I felt stupid: not once had I thought it might be concern for my well-being that caused Sorin to keep his distance. He had kissed my head and cheeks numerous times, held my hand, and lain beside me for days now. "Well, I'm not a fragile little teacup that can be so easily broken." I said it with a lack of empathy for what he was trying to express.

He slammed the counter with his fist again, and I heard another cracking sound. His eyes narrowed and his brows gathered. "Mia … that was with little effort. If I were to let my guard down … if we were to even try …" His voice trailed off, and he looked down at the broken pieces of teacup on the countertop. His face softened. "You could easily end up in the hospital." He brushed all the pieces into a pile. "I am not about to give in to … a situation where you could be physically hurt because of me. I will not allow it." His voice was gentle and soft.

I felt myself relax, and I stepped forward to collect the pieces and dispose of them. "Your pushing me away hurts me, Sorin." It was an honest statement that I voiced without regret.

"Well, I can live with your having hurt feelings much more easily than with your having broken bones—or worse." He said it with deep conviction.

I picked up the few pieces of teacup, and one cut my palm. "Ouch!" I complained. I dropped the broken porcelain again. Opening my hand, a thin red line appeared. I looked at Sorin, deciding it could be an opportunity. His eyes focused on the small cut. I didn't want to believe it was impossible to share some level of intimacy with him. I lifted my palm to him. "You have my permission, Sorin." His eyes met mine briefly, only to return to my palm. He cradled my hand, still hesitant. "Kiss the hurt away," I whispered. His lips lowered to my palm. A soft kiss, followed by his lips parting and a gentle trace of his tongue. I shuddered, and he stopped, withdrawing to clean the countertop completely of the debris.

I turned and retrieved a small bandage from a drawer. I again thought of him fresh out of the shower. I would have been content with a few kisses and feeling his arms around me. It had been years since I shared myself with a man; I told myself that a little while longer would be fine. I would not rush things, and eventually Sorin would give in. He scowled at me as he threw away the cup, the pieces clattering lightly in the trash.

"So kissing leads to broken bones, is that what you are trying to convince me of?" I challenged, my eyebrows rising.

He sat back down, his head tilted slightly, and his eyes circled me. I waited for his observation. "I no longer care to continue discussing this subject with you, Mia." His arms rested in front of him, and he forced a smile. Then, in an upbeat voice, he added, "I see you accepted the offer to paint for Mr. Szurpicki."

Annoyed, I turned to get a new teacup. "You are horrible at changing the subject, Sorin. Has anyone ever told you—" I stopped short, realizing I hadn't told him that information. I spun back to face him. "I didn't tell you I accepted the job offer. Those canvases could be for the coffee shop or my personal use. How did you know?" I placed the second teacup on the counter between us.

"I overheard you agree to meet with him, and the supplies led me to believe you accepted his offer," he said matter-of-factly.

Thinking of my lunchtime call, I looked toward the guest room and then back at him. "You never left, did you?" I said accusingly. "You have been here this whole time." I wasn't upset that he had been, just surprised that I had called out to him and received no response.

He shifted uneasily on the stool. "I promise you I intended on leaving. You were so unhappy by the end of the evening. I thought some distance was needed." He said it all quietly.

"But?" I asked, butterflies starting to stir inside me again.

"But as I stood at the patio door about to leave you … if only for the day … the mere thought was inconceivable. I did leave the house last night, parked my SUV a few blocks away, and then walked back without your realizing it." His voice had turned silken by the end of his confession. My head was starting to feel light, and I tried to fight it. Sorin continued, his voice a low purr. "If I could live the rest of my life and never be more than a moment from you … I would die content, Mia." A slight move of my tongue against the roof of my mouth confirmed all he said was true. His eyes looked over me slowly, and he made no attempt to hide it.

My head lightened further, and my knees started to feel weak. "I called out to you last night … and you didn't come." My words slurred.

"I could hear you did not really want me … last night." He slowly stood and circled the island between us. Sorin's eyes finally met mine. "Have you given any thought to … continue living?" He paused a few feet in front of me.

It took everything I had to utter a simple word. "Yes," I breathed weakly.

A grin played on his lips. "And what have you decided, Mia? … Tell me." His voice caressed my skin, and I struggled to keep from swaying.

"The thought of … living is becoming … highly considered," I said meekly.

His grin grew, and he closed the space between us. "Have you thought of accepting my offer to extend this life of yours … to spend the rest of your days with me?" My knees buckled, and I could no longer stand. Sorin's hands were instantly on my hips, steadying me. His eyes held mine in that same hypnotic gaze he used whenever he wanted something. I fought speaking, irritated at how easily I offered information in moments like this. His face became a little determined as I resisted complying so quickly. "Mia, tell me. … You want to." He sounded so self-assured. My own voice screamed inside my head, telling me not to give in so easily. "Tell me you will eventually agree to become mine … in every way," he persisted. His tongue slowly moistened his lips. "And I will be yours."

Sorin's hands slipped over the waist of my jeans and rested just under my shirt. The simple act of his hands touching my skin made me whimper. I wanted to scream yes, to throw myself against him. I opened my mouth to speak, knowing I would agree to anything he requested. He softly chuckled, and I squeezed my eyes shut, willing myself to snap out of this beautiful haze. I took a few deep breaths as my heart pounded, resounding in my ears. His fingers played gently at my sides.

I had to do or say something to show I could no longer be manipulated. Even if it was with mostly innocent intentions. I opened my eyes, fluttering my lashes, and reached out, grabbing his sweater. "Sorin," I breathed, hoping to sound incoherent. I clung to his sweater and pulled him closer.

He chuckled. "Yes, Mia?"

His confidence was annoying. It cleared any lingering clouds that filled my head. My eyes looked at his ice-blue pools of light, and without a second thought, I said, "Kiss me, and I will tell you." There was no wavering in my voice.

His hands instantly left my sides, closing around my fingers, which only dug deeper into the folds of fabric between them. The smug expression quickly drained from his face. We stood staring at one another. I didn't expect him to kiss me, no matter how badly he wanted an answer. I knew he wouldn't. I said it only to prove a point, to feel like I still had some control over my actions.

His fingers gently tried to uncurl mine. But he was unsuccessful; I wasn't about to make this easy for him. "I explained avoiding intimacy, Mia. … It is for your well-being." He said it with a voice full of compassion that I assumed was supposed to affect me.

If he wanted to test me, I was willing to play along. "It is just a kiss, Sorin. … Indulge me, and I will tell you all my secret thoughts." I spoke as seductively as I could manage in that moment.

His body tensed, and he straightened his back, which forced his chest out. His fingers again attempted to release my grip; this time, he used more force. I winced and pressed myself against him. It caused the desired response. Sorin's fingers stopped their assault, and a light moan escaped him. His eyes lowered to my lips, and for a brief moment, I thought he would kiss me after all. But the thought was fleeting. His face twisted into an expression of complete frustration, and his fingers tore mine from his sweater. I flinched but kept myself from yelping at the sharp discomfort. He released my hands in midair, and they fell to my sides. Sorin's jaw tightened, and he took a step back, putting some distance between us.

Quickly forgetting about my pain, I boldly smiled. "It's aggravating when someone toys with you. … Now you know how I have felt." My voice was a little above my normal tone.

He attempted a retort. "Mia, I do not ju—"

But I interrupted him midsentence. "And it's not fair, Sorin!" I said that even louder.

A look flashed across his face, and he exclaimed, "If both partners can equally influence one another, it is fair, Mia!" It was clear that he instantly regretted the information he had so freely given.

It took me a few minutes to comprehend the full meaning of what he had said. But if I understood correctly, given what he'd explained to me before, he was saying that I could make him feel all the things I had felt during the past week. My mind raced instantly. Was it really possible to fill his head with clouds and make him feel that he had lost all control of his will?

Sorin began to pace around a small area of the kitchen. I struggled to remember his earlier explanation. Something about his blood present in me giving him the ability to affect me, feel what I felt. I watched him continue to pace. He looked at me out of the corner of his eye.

I looked away, concentrating on my thoughts. He was only able to affect me because some part of me wanted it to be so. I had wanted the world to darken around me, wanted the pain to ease. And just now, he had proved it true again. Some part of me wanted to tell him all the things I had thought when I believed he was absent. But the small part of me that held a reservation was enough for me to keep from pouring my heart out. So I still had free will when I wanted to. I smiled as all the pieces fit. Sorin had bitten me days before, and a light kiss of my cut palm had just transpired. He had promised no permanent bond would result from such a small amount of blood. But Anya had clearly detected something between us. My stomach growled, bringing me out of my deep thoughts.

Sorin stopped pacing, turned, and scowled at me. He tilted his head and looked me over, his scowl intensifying. I ignored him, pouring hot water from the kettle to brew the tea I had started earlier. I went to the refrigerator and pulled a container from the black bag. The kitchen was still as I heated up the spaghetti. Only the clang of pans and a plate on the counter broke the silence. I thought of my colors, wondering what they currently looked like. I made up my mind I would test my suspicions of being able to control him by the end of the night. But I figured scheming under Sorin's glare wasn't the best way to go about it.

I stirred the pasta a few times and turned off the heat. I plated a generous portion and sat across from him. He looked at me, and I could somehow tell from his expression and body language exactly what was going through his head. He was trying to figure out if I had put it all together. I took a large bite and smiled. He must have known he'd said too much. Sorin was just apprehensive about what I would do next with that information. For the past week, I'd felt helpless in response to everything happening around me. Even my own body betrayed me at times. The sense of power or even the possibility of gaining some control over my life was well overdue. I took another bite; I couldn't remember spaghetti ever tasting so good. A feeling of pride washed over me. "This pasta is amazing. ... Did I ever thank you for dinner?" I couldn't recall.

His face softened just a little. "No," he said simply.

I stood up to pour more hot water into my teacup, which now held lukewarm tea. "That was terribly rude of me. ... Well, thank you for dinner. It is delicious." I overexaggerated the words.

"It won't work, Mia. ... Whatever ideas are filling your head." His tone was now firm and accusing.

I poured the water into my cup and then set the kettle back on the stove. I lifted a shoulder. "I don't know what you're talking about." I didn't bother to sound convincing as I sat back down.

"A moment ago your mind was occupied with multiple thoughts. Do not think you can hide your emotions from me, Mia. The colors surrounding you right now ... I have seen them before. Only now I understand their meaning. You are up to no good." His voice was different.

I stopped eating, trying to figure out what the difference was. "Keep talking," I said quickly. Sorin looked at me, puzzled. "Describe what I look like to you right now ... the colors you see." That was the first thing I could think of.

Sorin tilted his head and his eyes moved around me. "You still have darkness around you. ... But closer to you than the dark gray is a mixture of green and blue."

I imagined a teal color, and then I realized what was different. "Your accent ... it has faded," I said sadly. "You're losing your accent. ... I loved it." I was suddenly unhappy.

He reached across the counter and lovingly placed a hand over mine. "Mia ... I've told you it would eventually cease. It's nothing I can control; it just happens." He was using contractions more often too. He smiled lightly. "So you loved my accent?" His expression had softened even more.

Concluding that the scheming could wait till later, I looked down at his hand over mine, recalling how good he looked wearing only a towel. My eyes rose from his hand, and I let my gaze settle on his body. He wore his usual layers of dark-colored clothes, but it was easy for me to imagine him shirtless. My eyes drifted down his chest to his flat stomach.

Sorin's hand slowly retreated across the smooth marble between us, bringing me out my reverie. His posture stiffened, and his eyes avoided mine. I knew the colors surrounding me announced all that I thought and felt. I resolved to own my colors rather than try to fight them. My thoughts returned to him in the bathroom doorway. I had caught him off guard, even though Sorin had proved his keen sense of hearing. "I didn't think vampires could be surprised," I said. "I mean you were very ... deer caught in headlights." I tried not to smile.

"I had heard you leave earlier in the day, and my mind was otherwise occupied when you returned." A light shrug from his shoulders, and he continued. "I'm no different than you when it comes to the senses, Mia. Sometimes when you are concentrating on one thing so intensely … something else may be overlooked. It is rare for me, so do not expect history to repeat itself." His tone was strong, but I suspected it was a front.

I pushed. "So what had you so distracted?" I waited but did not count on an honest answer.

Sorin looked away, at some point over my head, and his vision fixed on something unimportant. "I may have to take a trip away for a day or two." His voice lacked any emotion, and his face was blank.

Bewildered, my stomach flipped and my heart sank. "You just said you didn't want to spend a moment away from me. Then, mere minutes later, you are talking about being gone for a day or two. If you need to go somewhere, fine. … Take me with you." I didn't want to be away from him for so long. A single night had been difficult, despite my trying to deny it. A day or two … ! I couldn't bear to even think about it.

He kept his gaze focused elsewhere. "It is not a trip of leisure, Mia. … It is becoming necessary." A few lines formed on his brow. "I need to spend the day away from you. … For my survival and for your safety."

His eyes locked with mine, and I swallowed, understanding what he was struggling to say. My heart tightened. He would be doing, with another person, something I considered to be so intimate, and it crushed me. I knew it was essential, but the thought sickened me. "You said you did not have to eat very often," I argued, pushing my plate away as I lost my appetite.

He nodded. "I also admitted to its being quite some time since my last meal." He leaned forward. "I have put it off for days now, and with each one that passes, it affects me more. Awareness of my surroundings is not what it should be. You proved that today. I neglected to address my need before arriving here. ... But if I continue to postpone it, I cannot promise to restrain myself around you." His eyes moved to my deserted plate of food. "Please try to eat more regularly, Mia. ... You're not helping my predicament." He smoothly left his seat and crossed the kitchen. Just before the dining room entrance, he said over his shoulder, "I am only trying to respect your wanting to decide your future. ... Don't make it more difficult than it already is."

I didn't stop him. I forced down a few more bites of food, and then I washed and dried the dishes, taking my time. With Sorin gone, I could think of anything I wanted to, without the concern of his watching me critically. I wondered if we could truly have a future together. It seemed there was a constant strain between us. We took turns hurting each other, usually unintentionally. The apologies were never ending. Every day it was another emotional battle; tension only increased as time passed. I imagined if I had met Sorin in another time or place, it would have been easy to have a life together. It would be less complicated if he weren't a vampire. Then I realized it was because he was a vampire, because he had crossed paths with my mother years before, that our lives were intertwined now.

I shut off the lights and ascended the stairs.

Chapter 3

Weak candlelight spilled from my room into the hallway. Sorin lay in my bed, waiting patiently.

Tired from not sleeping the day away, I yawned as I crossed to my dresser.

"Come to bed and rest, Mia." His voice, so soothing, beckoned to me. It was still a couple of hours before sunset. I opened my bottom dresser drawer to get some pajamas. Instantly, I opted for less clothing. It was warmer in the house than it had been before, and I was about to test exactly how much power I really had over Sorin. I took the pajama bottoms, knowing he was watching me. I closed the bottom drawer and opened the top one. I carefully removed an almost-sheer black camisole and lacy underwear. I rolled them into the pajama bottoms, trying to conceal them. I sensed his gaze burning into me but didn't care. I felt determined to break through the wall he repeatedly put up at the last minute. The desire to experience Sorin in a way he insisted was dangerous overtook me. I wanted to feel his skin under my fingertips. I needed to know something other than pain and frustration could transpire between us.

I turned to the bathroom, making sure to avoid eye contact. I combed my hair and brushed my teeth. Taking off my clothes and donning the camisole and underwear, my heart increased its rhythm. So many scenarios played out in my head, but I couldn't possibly know what would actually happen. I looked in the mirror and still did not care for my reflection. Had it not been for a couple of real meals today and a confidence boost, I wouldn't have considered trying what I was about to do. Just before leaving the bathroom, I visualized finally kissing Sorin, imagined tasting him on my lips. Unable to wait any longer, I craved his silver-blue eyes on me as the candlelight danced off of them. Leaving my clothes and pajama bottoms in a pile on the floor, I shut off the bathroom light. Inhaling deeply as I crossed the doorway, I stepped into the bedroom.

All breath left my body as my eyes met Sorin's. They were not a silvery blue as predicted, but instead, a deep vibrant purple. His fists were full of black satin at his sides. His back to the wall behind him, perfectly still. My heart was pounding, exhilarated. As I stood before him, scarcely covered, urgency grew inside me to join him. I took small steps, watching his response. He wanted to flee but felt trapped before me. Finally realizing how much control over him I really had, I moved closer. I wanted this; I needed to be touched. A little comforting and reassurance was my only goal. I told myself I didn't want more than that. I stepped to the foot of the bed, and Sorin pressed himself harder against the wall behind him.

"Please, Mia ... I do not wish to fight." His voice was a deep plea that only encouraged me more.

"No fighting ... just a little experiment." My voice was quiet as every nerve in my body screamed. I moved the satin sheet back and swiftly pulled the comforter underneath it toward my feet. Now only a thin sheet lay over Sorin.

His eyes fell from my face to my body, roving over my body. "Don't force me to leave you as I did last time, Mia. ... You felt completely rejected, and I do not want to experience that again."

His confession made my stomach knot. "Last time?" I said, thinking out loud. I knew he was talking about the night when, thinking he had left for good, I had almost ingested a handful of pills. A mixture of hurt and confusion filled me now. "You knew I was coming to your room?" I asked softly.

"I could feel the pain you felt, then the determination for an escape. I thought if I left … I thought the rejection would hurt less if I wasn't there to turn you away. My own restraint was slowly fading, and I was not sure I had the strength to say no, so I slipped outside. Thankfully not too far away, since your emotions drastically changed upon finding an empty room." His eyes met mine, and I slowly crept into the bed at his feet.

"What's different this time, Sorin? … You could have left before I stepped out of the bathroom." I wondered how much he would tell me.

"It was not like this so many nights ago, Mia. I had not just tasted your blood before that … almost encounter." He slowly shook his head.

"Why does that affect the result?" I suspected the answer but wanted him to explain further.

Without delay, he answered. "My blood has been in your system your whole life, Mia. I have felt your emotions and feelings only when they are overwhelming, due to how long ago my blood entered you. I can influence your moods or decisions only because they are what you really want. It is the same the other way around … only amplified because it was so recent. Your blood so newly in my system makes it difficult for me to refuse anything you want. In return, your feelings and emotions may not be your own. Giving your blood for my kind is an ultimate surrender. It can affect you mentally, physically. … It is a pure trust you put in someone's possession. A trust that should never be given freely … or taken without consent. We're both too fragile to commit to such a bond right now. A small amount of your blood will not guarantee anything permanent. The effects will decrease in a day or two."

I smiled lightly. "Anything else?"

His eyes moved over my body. "You were not hungry ... as you are now. That night it was desperation that surrounded you, not desire." His voice had a strain to it, and I loved it. I could no longer keep my distance from him. I slowly crawled to his lap. I placed my legs on either side of his, resting just above his knees. My hands rested on his shoulders and I gently ran them down his arms. Even through his sweater I could feel every muscle flexed. Sorin's hands each still held a fistful of bedding. I considered trying to pry open his clenched fists, but I was concerned the black satin would pay the price. I sighed; there was no current possibility of removing his sweater and shirt.

"Just relax," I whispered, slumping slightly so our eyes met.

"Mia ... please cease." A beautiful plea to stop hung in the air as I leaned forward to kiss him. He turned his head away, exposing his jawline, and I kissed it, giving the curve of it a soft bite. A throaty moan escaped Sorin, sending chills through my body. His usual scent of sandalwood tickled my nose.

I raised my lips to his ear. "It's okay ... I just want a kiss." I thought of the silky voice he had used on me and tried to mimic it. I brought my hands to his chest and smiled as I felt no heart beating under my palms. My own heart was pounding, and I wished to be rewarded with that response from him. His jaw was tense and still turned away from me. I backed away. His eyes were closed, and I longed to see the fiery purple I had only experienced a glimpse of.

Taking a deep breath, I willed myself to make this work. I slowly exhaled, focusing on Sorin. I kept my left hand on his chest while I cupped the left side of his face with my right. "Look at me." I spoke quietly but firmly, gently caressing his cheek with my thumb. Another rumble left him, an affirmation that I was being heard. "Sorin, please look at me." I continued in my slow sultry voice. His head finally turned to me, and he opened his eyes. I should have been frightened; his eyes were ablaze. The fiery purple when the candles danced over them looked wild, animalistic. I could see an internal war behind them. Determination surged through his body. "You want this also … I can feel it. I'll be fine, Sorin. I am not a fragile teacup so easily broken." I tried to reassure him. Help the last little reservation he had melt away.

I leaned toward him, and this time he didn't turn away. I kept eye contact as long as I could. I moistened my lips and teased them against his. Sorin's mouth still held tension, so I repeated the motion. This time letting my lips linger just a moment longer. Without moving away too far, I begged one last time. "It's just a kiss. Let go, Sorin … don't deny me this." My heart leaped as his whole body relaxed. I no longer felt it necessary to restrain myself. I slipped my hand from his cheek to the base of his neck on the opposite side. I pressed my lips fully to his and sighed at how great it felt. My fingers rose up to entangle in his hair. My eyes closed as my fingers tightened into Sorin's sweater and hair simultaneously. I parted my lips and delicately traced the crease of his mouth. "I want to taste you, Sorin." The words left my lips as an intense request. He shuddered softly and opened his lips partially. I resumed kissing him. First his upper lip, followed by his lower. As I nibbled on it between my teeth, Sorin trembled again, but with more force this time. A sound left him, purely male and frustrated. My heart skipped a beat, and I went back to small delicate kisses, unconcerned. My eyes fluttered open to see his again briefly.

"Cease!" he rasped.

"Just a little more," I promised. "If you really are at my mercy, I want to fully enjoy it." I eased the tip of my tongue past his lips and played along his teeth, trying to part them. An unexpected sharp point caught my tongue, and I lightly yelped into Sorin's mouth. My eyes flew open as I drew back, raising my left hand to the pain instinctively. I tasted blood, metallic and bitter.

"Cease, Mia!" His raised voice had a frantic sound to it.

My right hand still held a fistful of hair in it. I tightened my grip and pulled his head back, moving my other hand to his face. I pinched his chin the way he had pinched mine so many times before. "I want to see," I gently demanded.

His mouth opened, and I lightly gasped as the candle's flame revealed pearly white fangs extended to the finest points. Sorin began to turn his head away, but I covered his mouth with mine before he could complete the effort. I roughly kissed him, raking my tongue against his fangs. If my blood fresh in his system was needed to make him more compliant, I was happy to give it. The pain barely registered, drowned out by endorphins and adrenaline rushing through my body. I gave no regard to the outcome as the metallic taste grew, oddly thrilling me. Any control he clung to immediately vanished.

Sorin's hand flew to my face, holding it to his as if he suddenly feared I might shrink away. As he kissed me back at last, I couldn't help wanting more than I had initially requested. I lowered my hands to his waist and slipped them under his shirt. I ached to explore his chest. A tortured moan was his reply. His right hand left my face and clamped down on my upper arm, trying to lift my hand from under his shirt.

"More," I breathed against his mouth. Plunging my tongue past his lips, I forced it into one of his fangs again. More slight pain, but I ignored it. Sorin's fingers dug into my upper arm, and I winced. I tried to pull my arm away to free myself. His hand swiftly followed my left arm to my wrist, just under his shirt, never completely letting go. His finger's tightened around my wrist, forcing it toward my own body. I quietly whined in protest. Fighting back, I tried to turn my wrist away. My right hand continued farther up his shirt, relieved he had yet to capture it. I pressed myself against him and moved my hand to the small of his back, trying to pull him to the bed beneath us. His fingers constricted around my wrist more aggressively. I cried out, but it was muffled by his mouth. This seemed to excite him, and his kisses became frenzied. Fear came over me, and I panicked. I twisted my wrist against his hold, jerking it as I tried to free myself.

Sorin froze as I moved back, opening my eyes. I looked into his eyes, trying to catch my breath. Right before me, the deep purple faded to the silvery blue, and complete horror filled his eyes. My blood ran cold, and I knew something was wrong.

"What?" I asked, afraid.

His eyes fell to my left hand, and he let it go. "You don't feel it?" he said, astonished. In a fluid movement he grabbed my sides, lifting me off him and placing me on the bed. In a blur, he was at my dresser, tearing through the drawers.

"What are you doing?" My voice was full of dread.

He started tossing clothes, dropping them next to me on the bed. "Your wrist!" he yelled. "It's broken! ... Hell, Mia, I can feel it. Why can't you?" He lifted a pair of jeans from the bed and rushed to the side I had moved to.

I bent my wrist, shrugging. "It's tender ... but that's to be expected from how tight you held it." I brushed the clothes away.

Ignoring my opinion, he straightened my legs so they draped over the edge of the bed. "I broke your wrist, Mia. ... You are going to the hospital this instant." Sorin slipped my jeans onto my legs and guided me off the bed to finish dressing me. He shook his head, frustrated. "You may not feel it yet, but you will."

I looked down at my wrist, not believing him. "You're wrong," I said, rolling my wrist to prove it. At a certain angle, pain shot through it. I cried out, surprised, but quickly tried to excuse it. "It's a little tender, that's all ... really." I attempted to keep any pain from showing on my face. I knew it wouldn't matter, and I bit my lip to keep from cursing.

"Hospital, Mia! Now!" he roared at me, and I flinched. He carefully maneuvered my injured hand through a T-shirt sleeve to finish dressing me. I looked at the alarm clock and saw it was still more than an hour before sunset.

I protested, dragging my feet while he led me to the doorway. "You can't go outside yet ... I can wait a little longer to leave." I figured my plea would mean little to him. He flung the bedroom door open and gave me a look that convinced me I wasn't even close to winning this battle. He walked me downstairs, and I gathered my keys and purse, careful not to bend my left wrist. I held it carefully against my chest. It was awkward using only one hand. I stepped to the front door and was about to try one final attempt at putting off my trip. But when I turned to face Sorin, he was gone. I looked upstairs, and he was only a few steps from entering my room.

I left, closing the door behind me, crushed. Again careful not to bump my hand, I climbed into my car. The hospital was just outside of town. I sat in the driveway awhile. It had ended so abruptly with Sorin, and now he blamed himself for my being hurt. We were both at fault for my injury. I had ignored his warnings, and he should have left before anything began. Before we knew it, a line had been crossed. He had held my wrist, but I had twisted it away.

Eventually I started the car, hoping my wrist wasn't really broken. I took my time driving, not looking forward to what was about to happen. I pulled into a parking spot and exited the car cautiously. I walked to the entrance and a sudden rush of déjà vu washed over me. I stopped as the doors automatically opened with a whoosh. They closed after a minute, only to open again instantly. My eyes watered, and I wanted to turn around.

A nurse came from behind the counter to inspect the door's strange malfunction. She noticed me and walked to my side, worry covering her face. She placed her hand on my back and led me through the doors. "Are you okay, sweetie? ... Can I help you?" The concern in her voice registered, and I blinked back tears.

"My wrist," I whispered. She looked down at the arm I held against my chest. "I think I hurt it," I explained.

The lobby was empty, and I looked around reluctantly, remembering that night not so long ago. She hurried behind the counter and picked up a clipboard containing papers for me to fill out. She started to escort me to a chair, and I pulled away from her. "Can I fill them out in the room, please?" I heard my voice crack, and she nodded yes.

I followed her down the hall and turned into the last room on my right. I sat in the empty chair and rested the clipboard on my lap. The nurse paused, and I looked up at her. "Yes?" I asked, wondering if there was something else.

"It will be a few minutes before the doctor is available, miss." Her voice held an odd tone, and she looked at my arm as she spoke.

I looked back down at the clipboard. "That's fine. Thank you." She shuffled backward out of the room and into the hallway. Once the door was closed, I wiped away the tears that filled my eyes. I had most of the papers filled out when a gentle tap on the door made me look up. In walked a doctor with perfectly combed salt-and-pepper hair. Wrinkles filled his forehead and the corners of his eyes. He introduced himself, smiling and holding out his hand. I shook it softly and weakly smiled back, noticing his hazel eyes lowering to my arm. He pulled a chair over and sat in front of me. I explained I had hurt my wrist and carefully moved it away from my chest. He inspected it, and I whimpered as he bent it.

"I'll order an X-ray," the doctor said, adding that a nurse would be in shortly with an anti-inflammatory and an ice pack.

I looked down at my wrist briefly to see it was swollen. The doctor left, and I finished the last few questions on the paperwork.

Another knock caught my attention. A different nurse walked in, slightly older than I. She was petite, had bright-blue eyes, and wore her blonde hair in a tight ponytail. She carried a long white ice pack and a little cup containing a large white pill. I held out my good hand and took the ice pack from her. I folded it around my wrist, laying it on my lap. I then took the cup from her and looked at the sink across the room.

I started to get up, but she held out her hand. "Oh no, no … I will get you a drink. Just sit there." She filled up a child-sized paper cup and returned to me. I swallowed the pill and set the empty cup aside. "Thank you," I said, clearing my throat. She threw the cup away and started to leave. At the last minute, she turned back to me. "Do you need me to call anyone for you?" The nurse's eyes moved over me, and her emphasis on *anyone* confused me. She had the same expression as the first nurse.

"I'm fine, really … just hurt my wrist."

She opened the door. "If you change your mind, I will be right down the hall." She finally left, and I rested my head against the wall behind me, trying not to think of anything.

A while later the X-ray technician wheeled the bulky machine through the door. His voice was light. "Did someone order an X-ray?" His face popped out from behind the machine. Short red hair and a few freckles on his nose. His smile quickly faded, and his tone lowered. "It will just take a minute to do the X-rays and then get them off to the doctor for you." He shut the door behind him.

"Thank you," I said automatically.

Lifting up his clipboard, he looked at it quizzically, and then looked back at me. "Just the wrist?" he stumbled over his words.

"Excuse me?" I responded, not understanding the question. The technician's eyes studied me in the same way that the nurses' had, and I felt annoyed. "Am I only taking an X-ray of your wrist?" he said, his voice low as he leaned in my direction.

Everyone was looking at me strangely and treating me like a child. My patience was wearing thin. "What does the order say?" I said rudely.

He put the paper down and explained what I needed to do. He delicately moved my wrist and placed it where needed. I turned away both times, not caring to see my swollen wrist. When the technician was done, he wheeled the machine out. No longer wishing to be polite, I failed to thank him.

The door shut, and I stood in the room, irritated. I was so angry with myself, knowing this was my doing. Sorin had warned me repeatedly, but I refused to listen. I started walking around the room. I crossed to the sink across the room. A splash or two of water on my face would distract me. I turned a knob with a pretty cerulean swirl on it. Holding my aching hand against me, I passed the fingers of my other hand under the water to test it. My eyes drifted to the mirror in front of me. Seeing my reflection, I gasped, barely recognizing myself. The staff had reason to look at me the way they did. My hair was a tousled mess, my lips were bright pink and swollen as a result of Sorin's rough kisses. Dried blood rested in the corner of my mouth. Light bruises traced the bottom of my right cheek. My eyes lowered to my injured arm held against my chest. Another bruise much worse peeked out from the edge of my sleeve above my elbow. My eyes began to water. I looked like someone had beaten me. I was angry with Sorin for forcing me to leave the house in this condition. Then realized I had been here for over an hour now. The bruises were only getting worse.

I did the best I could to improve my appearance. Desperate to look less disheveled, I smoothed my hair back and considered putting the ice pack over my cheek. I pulled on my sleeve, trying to lower it over the bruise as I returned to the chair. Slowly, I undid the Velcro on the ice pack and gently slid my wrist from inside, cringing at the immediate pain that occurred. More tears formed, falling down my cheek. The ice pack had covered my wrist, but now that I'd moved it, I could see an unusually shaped discoloration. I knew it was from Sorin's tight grip on my wrist.

A light tap on the door gave me just enough warning to slip my hand back into the ice pack. I was wiping away my tears when the doctor entered, carrying a laptop under his arm and holding a CD case in his hand. "I have your X-ray here. ... Should we take a look?" He said it with a hint of what I now understood was suspicion.

I shrugged, feeling defeated and ashamed. I moved my right arm over my chest and covered the bruise above my elbow. The doctor inserted the CD into a slot in the laptop, and an image soon appeared on the screen. He looked at the screen, crossing his arms. His body blocked my view, and I didn't bother to look around him. He leaned in close to inspect the X-ray.

The pretty blonde nurse stepped in and picked up the clipboard with my information. As she passed the doctor, she slowed to look at the X-ray onscreen, causing him to nod for her to leave. But not before a look of pity crossed her face.

I massaged my forehead and took a deep breath, trying to remain calm.

The doctor turned around and leaned against the sink near him. "So ... ready for the verdict?" He raised his eyebrows, with his arms still crossed.

"Sure," I said quietly.

"The good news is ... it is not broken. Just a hairline fracture." He shifted his weight and continued. "How did you say you hurt your wrist again?"

I couldn't possibly explain it. "I fell," I said, both of us knowing it was a lie. "Fell?" he said, echoing me. "And the bruises?" he pressed.

"It was a bad fall." I looked down at the floor, ready to be done, for the questions to end.

The doctor stayed silent for a few minutes. Disappointment covered his face when I looked back up at him. "I can't help you if you won't let me, miss." He said it with touching concern.

"Really, I don't need any help. ... Thank you." I sighed. "So what do I do about the ... hairline fracture?" I stood, hoping to make it clear I was ready to be done.

He turned, popped the CD from the drive, put it back in the case, and flipped the laptop closed. The doctor then took a pen and prescription pad from his pocket. "Here is a prescription for an anti-inflammatory." He ripped off the page and scribbled again. "Here is one of for a pain reliever. Read all the warnings and side effects with this one. No driving or operating machinery; the usual. See your regular doctor to make sure it heals correctly." He ripped off the second page, put both prescriptions on the counter near the sink, picked up his laptop, and walked to the door. "The nurse will be in to wrap your wrist and help you with anything else you may need."

I knew what he was insinuating and lowered myself back down to my chair. He left, and I wanted to scream. A few minutes later, the nurse returned, pushing a small cart in front of her. "Let's get your wrist wrapped up." Her smiled didn't reach her eyes. She moved the chair to sit in front of me. Carefully removing the ice pack she fussed at the sight before her. "Oh, honey." Her words rushed out. "I'll give you a card. ... There's a place you can go, and—"

I interrupted her. "I'm okay, really. ... Thank you."

She opened her mouth to argue further. I gave up trying to convince everyone things weren't as they seemed; their minds were set, so there was no point in my trying. "I'm not going back to him ... I promise." I blurted out. Her mouth closed. "I will be moving in with my sister, and I'll have the police present when I collect my things," I added, hoping something would eventually appease her. I tried to sound convincing.

She turned back to my wrist and wrapped it. Then she pulled out a plain black sling and pushed the cart away. After helping me get the sling on, she stepped to the counter near the sink and picked up the prescriptions. Pulling a business card from her pocket, she placed it on top the papers. I thanked her for everything and reached out to take the papers she handed me. She squeezed my good hand as I took the papers from her. The nurse wished me well and encouraged me to call the number on the card.

I left the hospital as quickly as I could and took the prescriptions to the pharmacy down the road.

Chapter 4

It was dark by the time I arrived home. I opened the front and stepped inside. The house was dark with the exception of the dimmed foyer light above me. The fear that Sorin might have left hadn't occurred to me until that moment. I stood still and listened closely. Nothing. "Sorin?" I whispered weakly. I looked to the kitchen, and by the time I decided to go upstairs he had rushed down and stood at the bottom of the steps. I looked at him, overcome by my emotions. He waited, clearly not sure what to do. I dropped everything I held, and it all clattered to the floor. I burst into tears and ran to him. Throwing myself into his arms, completely forgetting about my hurt wrist, I cried out in pain as I slammed against him.

"Mia!" he lightly scolded me and wrapped his arms around me protectively.

Sorin was gentle, and I buried my head in his chest. "It was awful!" I cried, and the tears only increased as I relived the past few hours. "I had to walk through the same hospital doors. ..." I gasped for air. "Have you seen me? ... I look beaten. ... They thought I had been abused." I sucked more air in. "My wrist is really starting to hurt, and I had to do it all without you."

He kissed the side of my head and tried to calm me. "*Shhh,*" he said, trying to soothe me.

We just stood there together, and gradually my tears lessened. I eased away from him and made eye contact. "Make it better, Sorin. ... Please."

The moment the request left my lips Sorin stepped away from me.

Confused, he asked. "What are you asking me to do?"

I had thought it obvious. "I don't know. ... Say something. ... Do whatever you do. Make it better. ... It really hurts."

He shook his head, refusing to grant my simple request. "You are hurt because you insisted on doing something I warned you not to do." His hands balled at his sides. "Then, after my repeatedly telling you to stop ... you continued." He shook his head, and his voice rose. "This has been torture waiting here for you. Knowing I hurt you, Mia. ... I should have pushed you away earlier. Left when you refused to heed my warnings." I couldn't believe what he was saying. "You cannot expect me to simply make it better. ... It truly hurts me to say this ... but you need a reminder of the consequences when you have no regard for your safety."

My head spun. I was exhausted and in pain. He didn't care if I suffered. "I know what I did!" I yelled. "I admit I completely ignored your warnings. But I thought you were exaggerating. I didn't expect to get hurt. ... Maybe a part of me didn't care it was a possibility." I took a deep breath before continuing.

Sorin interjected, correcting me. "Broke, Mia ... I broke you ... and I—"

"It is a hairline fracture, Sorin!" I cut in, storming past him and up the stairs. Over my shoulder I yelled, "I'm not beyond repair! No thanks to you. ... You could make it well again. But no, you want me to suffer." I reached the top of the stairs and turned to my room, continuing to say aloud everything that was on my mind. "You think this is a lesson to learn!" I stopped just before my door and turned to face him. "Or maybe you think this will slow me down!"

I spun around and entered my room, slamming on the light. Looking at my bed, I just wanted to lie down. Sorin entered the room with a cold glass of water in one hand and two large white pills in the other. He held them out for me. "I can tell you have not taken them yet. ... Go ahead. I feel how much it hurts." I filled my mouth with some water and passed back the glass in exchange for the pills. I swallowed them, still unhappy. "I don't want to take the pain pills, Sorin. ... We both know how I respond medication." I did not enjoy how the sleeping pill many nights ago had made me feel.

Sorin set down the glass of water and led me to the side of the bed that was normally his. "That was a sleeping pill, Mia; this is for pain. Contrary to what you believe, I do not want you to suffer." He knelt over, slipping my sandals off my feet and laying them neatly on the floor.

"That's even worse!" I complained. "I will feel drunk and incoherent. I won't make any sense." I thought of the job I had just accepted. A colorful profanity filled the room, and Sorin's head jerked up. "I have six paintings due in two ... three weeks. Plus, the mama bears want me to do another series for the coffee shop. How am I supposed to—"

Sorin gently placed a finger over my lips. "*Shhh* ... do not worry about all of it right now." His voice was caring as he helped me slowly lie back on the bed. He turned his back to me, and I was puzzled for a moment. Then he made an irritated sound.

My nerves were shot, and my patience was already worn thin. "You have seen me almost nude, Sorin. You can help me undress. ...

Really. I promise to behave if that is what you want to hear." I started to fumble with my jeans.

He turned and cautiously removed them. I watched his face, but he showed no sign of thoughts other than taking care of me. He pulled the sheet to my waist. I sat up, undoing the sling over my shoulder, and pulled at my shirt. Sorin hesitated, but then he tenderly removed it. His eyes fell on my bruised arm, and guilt filled his face.

I looked down at my wrist and delicately touched it with my fingers. "Pretty amazing what some endorphins and adrenaline can block a person from feeling," I said, trying to lessen some of his guilt. He placed a pillow at my left side to prop my wrist up on, and I lightly smiled. "Really, it didn't hurt."

He shook his head. "No, it hurt. You just refused to feel it."

I lay back, trying to relax, and my stomach growled. Sorin didn't bother to excuse himself. He was a blur out the door, and I knew he would be back in a minute or two with a meal. "Cold spaghetti is fine. … Please don't bring me a lot of food." I said it just above my normal tone, hoping he would listen. Surprisingly, he took his time downstairs.

Once back, he put pillows behind me and placed the cherrywood tray over my lap. "Supper in bed. I can honestly say it is a first for me. Thank you."

Sorin lightly grinned. "Actually, I would have insisted. Between your hunger affecting mine and the sound of the human stomach growling …" He tried to find the right words.

"I get it," I said quickly. "It's loud, disturbing, disgusting … one or all of the above. Don't worry; I won't take it personally." I started to eat, but after a few bites, the base of my neck started to tingle. "Damn, that was fast," I mumbled my complaint. I knew the effects would quickly intensify. I did not normally take prescription medication. Even over-the-counter medicines were a last resort for me. I had experienced the removal of an impacted molar right after graduation from high school, and I remembered what it was like to be on pain medication. I would soon be slurring my speech and tripping over my own feet if I attempted to walk. Worst of all, I would not be able to hold a conversation. I hurried my eating, thinking the effects wouldn't be so bad if I put some food in my stomach.

Sorin sat on the bed, watching me, and then he took the tray away after I finished the plate of spaghetti and drank a glass of milk. He took it all down to the kitchen, returning just a moment later. The tingling was slowly crawling up the back of my head, and I plopped back against the pillows behind me. Sorin lit a few candles and shut off the overhead light.

"I don't like this," I stated as he moved around the room slowly.

"Well, I am not enjoying this feeling either." His words sounded a little funny. I turned my head against the pillow so I could look at him. Sorin was rubbing the back of his neck. My head was fuzzy, and it took a minute for it to register why his behavior seemed abnormal. I quickly sat up, and the room tilted. Sorin stepped to the bed and sat down, quickly raising both hands to his head. I chuckled. "You feel this ... your head feels all fuzzy, doesn't it?" I leaned on my right hand, afraid of falling back.

"Yes, Mia, unfortunately I will be extra-sensitive to what you feel for the next day. A consequence that I must experience for tasting your blood." He massaged the sides of his head more aggressively.

"Is it like that for you when … you taste any human?" I wondered aloud.

"No, just you, because I have shared myself with you." He paused and then continued, saying more than what I think he normally would have as a result of the pills' effects. "It has been so long since you were exposed to my blood … so I only feel extreme physical responses or emotions. It would be so much worse had you tasted mine today. I would feel exactly what you are currently. Not the dulled version. But because … I took from you days ago … you felt exactly what I did when Anya struck me. For that reason alone, I should have pushed you away and not allowed you to kiss me as you did, Mia." He lowered his hands. "It will pass … it is just so soon after kissing you … I should be more aware of my emotions for your sake." He started to struggle for words himself. "It was selfish of me. The more we exchange blood, the more the drive and desire to complete a bond will increase. So no more kissing. … It is for the best."

My eyes grew heavy, and the combination of everything crashed down on me. I crumpled back into the bed, giggling lightly. "Kissing you," I responded. "Kisses … red kisses … deep metallic kisses." I rambled but couldn't stop myself. I closed my eyes. "I loved your crimson kisses, Sorin. I don't care how much it hurts now. Your mouth was so—" His lips pressed into mine, and I sucked in a surprised breath. His lips didn't move, just stayed pressed against mine. He was silencing me, not kissing me. I attempted to raise my hand to his face, but it wobbled in the air. My coordination was starting to fail me.

He pulled away and lay on the bed next to me. "Please go to sleep." It was a gentle plea, and a half laugh shook my body.

The prickles and cobwebs continued. Normally I would have fought it. But knowing he was feeling everything, even if only a little, gave me a mildly sadistic satisfaction. Darkness quickly sucked me in, and I was lost within it.

I didn't wake up until lunchtime the next day. My head pounded and my wrist throbbed. I stirred, and Sorin instantly guided me up, holding two pills in his hand. I pushed them away. "Which one is for the swelling?" I asked. "Because it's the only one I will take." I moaned and rubbed the back of my neck. I caught a glimpse of the clock on my dresser. "What time is it?" I asked in disbelief.

"Past noon," Sorin said, trying to give me both pills again. I shoved his hand away.

"I told the mama bears I would come by today!" I complained. "And I need to start on the paintings. How could you have let me sleep so late?" I tried to move from the bed, but he caught me by the waist.

"Slow down, Mia."

I turned my head toward him. He let go, holding out one white pill. I didn't have time to be suspicious. I quickly swallowed it and slowly slipped from the bed. I picked up the sling that had fallen to the floor. I set it on the bed and pulled some clothes from my dresser. I caught a reflection of myself in the mirror, and stopped. My cheek looked even worse; the bruise had spread overnight. Between that and my arm in a sling, I knew that Jennifer, Gina, and Natalie would bombard me with questions. I walked to my side of the bed, and he eased to the side I had just abandoned to make room for me.

I slumped over and grabbed my phone. "I can't go to the coffee shop looking like this," I said sadly, more to myself than to Sorin. He squeezed my leg just above the knee in a show support. I called the shop, and Jennifer answered. I regretfully told her I was swamped with my painting work and wouldn't be able to make it out for a few days. She said she understood, but I clearly heard the disappointment in her voice. I said good-bye and tossed the phone down, irritated.

My wrist throbbed, and I decided to dull the pain, as I wouldn't be leaving the house. The glass of water sat on the nightstand next to me, along with a pile of crackers and the other pill. I swallowed the pill, looking back at Sorin while I ate the crackers. I hadn't realized it before, but he was lying on top of the comforter and sheet at the moment. It was warm in the house from changing the temperature. I wore only the black lace underwear and sheer camisole from the night before, but I felt perfectly comfortable. I looked down at myself, practically nude, and didn't feel uneasy in front of Sorin. He wore dark-gray pajama bottoms made of a thick material and a long-sleeved shirt.

I sighed and shook my head at his appearance. "So how warm does it have to get for you to … dress less?" I teased.

He didn't answer, just crossed his arms while a displeased look appeared on his face.

I walked to my dresser and put away the clothes I had pulled out. I grabbed a worn-out lightweight T-shirt that I often wore while painting. Laying it on top of the dresser beside me, I struggled to remove my camisole, turning to Sorin for help. He purposely moved slowly and kept silent, unhappy with my teasing. "I will behave. Just help me, please." I tried to look innocent.

He paused, tilting his head. "I really do not like the medications in you."

I stuck out my bottom lip, enjoying the disgust in his voice. "What's wrong?" I asked, curious. I reached out, taking his hand and guiding it to the edge of my camisole. He shot me a look of warning, and I let go. He raised his eyes to the ceiling and slowly lifted the camisole over my head.

Once it was a free, he turned his back to me. "The pills make you smell different, my head has a constant dull ache, and you are actually taking pleasure in guilting me into assisting you any way I can."

My eyes darted past him to the bathroom. He was right: all the pain I currently felt seemed overshadowed by a new sense of power. "I could use some help with a bath later." His body tensed, and I loved it. I stood, holding my injured arm against my bare chest, and reached for the T-shirt. I paused, considering whether to try to kiss Sorin.

"You said you would behave, Mia. Honor your word." His tone was another warning.

I looked down at my bruised arm, and any romantic notions melted away. I wondered if he even found me attractive right now. I imagined what he must think when he looked at me, seeing bruises left by his hands. I assumed the remorse was great and no longer hoped for any immediate affection. I picked up my T-shirt, carefully guided my left hand in, and then pulled the shirt over my head. I finally wiggled my good hand through the other sleeve and pulled down the shirt, covering myself. It was easier to dress than to undress.

Sorin retrieved the sling for my arm and assisted me with it. As he adjusted it, standing only inches from me, I caught him looking at my bruised arm. His face was devoid of any emotion, almost detached.

"Really … it doesn't hurt that much, Sorin." I caught his attention as he finished with the sling, stepping back. "I am sure it looks worse than it feels." He looked in my eyes, still silent, with no emotion on his face. "I swear, between the adrenaline and endorphins flooding my body while … I hardly felt a thing."

He said nothing, just walked past me to the doorway. "I think you can finish dressing yourself. I will meet you downstairs." He turned and left.

I removed my black lacy underwear and slipped on some cotton boy shorts. The attic always ran warmer than the rest of the house. Plus, all the windows were covered and there was no concern about being seen from outside. I started down the steps, and my head started to tingle. I recalled the previous night, and how I had rambled on about kissing Sorin. Then he had pressed his lips to mine to silence me. I smiled to myself and decided I would try to refrain from saying whatever I was thinking.

He was waiting for me in the kitchen. He had prepared sliced apples and a croissant for me; the plate sat on the counter. Sorin sat, staring off to the side. The only movement he made was when he rubbed his head every once in awhile, which always coincided with a reaction I felt from the medication. I tried to ignore its effects, especially how disconnected my head felt. By the time I was done eating, I felt like I was walking through a dream. I stumbled to the kitchen sink. I turned and saw Sorin quietly suffering from the same side effects. His eyes were glazed over, vacant. I took less pleasure in it now, and remembered he had commented that it passed quickly. I wondered if a physical distance would help. "I'm going to attempt to start my paintings. I'm sure it won't be easy. Any progress will be an accomplissmemt ... accomplishment." I moaned at the difficulty of pronouncing my words correctly.

Sorin finally looked at me, instantly sitting up from his hunched position. A hint of nervousness crept into his expression, and he looked toward the ceiling. He stood, starting in the direction of the stairs. I held out my good arm. "I can get upstairs myself, just sit back down." He rested a hand on the countertop in attempt to still what I figured was the same tilting feeling I was experiencing. "I can manage, thank you ... I'm not helpless." I started toward the dining room, my legs unwilling to completely leave the floor beneath me. "Just really discombobulated." I said it slowly, careful to pronounce my words correctly.

I continued to the attic, resting my hand on the railing as I reached the steps. After every few steps, I paused, trying to gather myself. At the top I considered turning to my room and lying down until the effects of the pain pill subsided a little, but I told myself I needed to at least start the process. Spread out the canvases, draw out a rough draft on each, and decide on colors. Determined, I proceeded to the attic steps. After another uncoordinated ascent, I entered the attic. My heart started pounding as I recalled the last time I was in this room. I turned the light on and saw blankets draped over the window. I hadn't thought to hang up curtains in the attic. That moment of answering the phone flashed before my eyes, and I started to cry. I looked at the floor, expecting to find the paint and brush I had dropped still there. But nothing lay before me. It was possible Aaron had cleaned it when he brought the paintings down for the deli owner the day after my parents' accident. More likely Sorin had done it. Clearly he had been spending time up here. It was warm and I was sure it felt good to him. If I didn't enjoy sharing a bed with him so much I would suggest moving one up here for him. I realized then that I had yet to see him sleep.

My new canvases lined the far wall, overlapping one another. I crossed the attic, choosing to spread out the canvases, desperate to be inspired or even motivated. I dragged my feet, my legs too heavy to lift. I moved the first canvas, almost as tall as I was. This was an awkward maneuver with only one hand. Sliding the canvas across the room, I set it along a different wall. Turning back for a second one, a small painting caught my eye. It was of me. I moved closer: an 11 x 14 close-up of me sleeping. I noticed the pearls around my neck in the painting. The last time I wore them was the day I buried my parents. The painting was like a picture from Sorin's mind just moments after seeing me for the first time. I knelt down to look closer at the details, and the edge of another painting peeked out. I moved the next new large canvas, and another painting of me leaned against the wall. It was larger than the first. I immediately began moving all my new blank canvases around, resting them along other walls in the room.

I had half of them moved when Sorin blurred past me and moved the rest of them. I lowered my body to the floor as he revealed that the entire wall had been lined with paintings of me. Tears filled my eyes as I looked from the first to the second then the third. "They are beautiful," I said, breathless. He stood next to me, offering to help me stand. My head was clouded and confused by it all. I gently pushed his hand away and wiped my tears. "Go," I whispered. I was overwhelmed, and it didn't help having Sorin hovering over me.

"I cannot tell ... are you unhappy?" he said, uncertain.

I shook my head slowly. "No … just go, please." I just wanted to be alone as I looked at the paintings. To see how he viewed me this past week, his perception. Sorin left, and I barely overheard a complaint about my medication affecting my colors.

As I heard the door close, I exhaled the breath I had caught in my chest. I wiped a few more tears and closed my eyes momentarily. Taking a deep breath, I tried to focus. I moved to the first painting and lifted it off the floor. I rested it on my legs to more closely inspect it. It was hard to see the brushstrokes, and I touched the pearls lightly. I placed it back and slid to the next one. It was painted in a totally different technique than the first, and the colors were bright and vivid. The first one was perfect, almost like a photograph, with colors true to life. The one I currently leaned over was millions of tiny spots and all primary colors. I was sitting in the corner of the sofa as if it were some leisurely afternoon. It would have been difficult for someone to see the beauty in the subject, but not the amazing pointillism technique. I ran my fingers over it delicately, all the tiny bumps jumping underneath my touch. The next held a darker mood. The colors were black, grays, and deep blues. I tilted my head, trying to figure it out. I saw a combination of circles, squares, diamonds, and other various shapes. I struggled to find the subject. I looked back at the first one from our first meeting, then the one from our second evening together. I looked at the third again, laying it on its side. I lifted my right hand and lay it over my chest as my heart began to ache. I starred at myself lying in Sorin's arms on the bathroom floor. At first glance, it was simply a young woman with masculine arms wrapped around her. There was a little of the bathroom floor's diamonds behind me. Looking at the painting, I realized the dark thoughts that I experienced that night had passed.

As much complication as Sorin had brought to my life, he had become my reason to continue. I turned back to the door, feeling the urge to call out to him. I slipped my hand from my chest to the floor and moved farther to my right.

The fourth canvas was large, with colors brushed in a crosshatch technique. I lightly smiled. This one was of me in the foyer before our night out. Just as all the paintings before it, my image filled most of the canvas. But his hand was tucking a rose behind my ear. I moved to the next and blushed. I was nude, lying nude on my side, facing away. Everything was black around me. The comforter below held no wine-colored roses. The black satin sheet draped over my hip. I remembered being a little warm that night and thinking Sorin had left. My lower legs peeked out from under the other side of the sheet. My cheeks warmed further as I wondered if that was the exact sight he had seen. Or if he had painted the sheet in for my modesty.

The last painting was the largest. I was surprised it hadn't stuck out from my new canvases. Filled with black and grays. Large bold strokes, a detailed garnet-colored rose near the corner. It was beautiful but puzzling. A delicate rose surrounded by chaos. I determined it must be a metaphor; artist interpretation or something. My head felt slightly better than before, and I figured Sorin was probably somewhere pacing. I called out to him, and by the time I finished his name, the door was creaking open. I sat on the floor, still trying to decipher his last painting. I twisted, facing him, and held my hand out for his. He walked to me and helped me up. I laid my head on his upper chest, wrapping my good arm around him. "I love them," I whispered. "And now I know what you do while I'm sleeping." I stepped back to look at him.

"This and watching television," he confessed.

Irritated with him for losing most of his accent, I responded with, "No more television."

He lightly smiled. "Mia, you speak in a northeastern American dialect. Considering you are the only person I am conversing with, it would have happened eventually." He ran his hand down my arm and took my hand. "So you love them, truly?" His smile grew a little more.

I repositioned my hand in his, turning back to the last paintings. "I could hardly see brushstrokes in a few." My vision continued down the line. "You have amazing range when it comes to your technique and style. Side by side, I would never guess they were by the same artist."

Sorin lightly chuckled. "I have lived many years and studied art around the world."

My eyes moved to the one of myself sleeping nude. "I won't ask if the sheet really happened to be lying … just right."

He wrapped an arm around me and pulled me back against him. I relaxed and laid my face against his. I felt him smile. "Yeah … that's what I thought." I finally looked down at the last painting we now stood just a foot or two from. "I do think this one is beautiful … I just don't understand a rose surrounded by a bunch of black and gray." I tried to say it gently.

He chuckled and stepped back, lightly lifting me along with him. "Do you see it now, Mia?" I looked at the bright rose and shrugged. He repeated the motion, lightly lifting me as he stepped back. I quietly gasped as I finally saw the painting in its entirety. "Sometimes we are too close to something to see the whole picture ... but a step back can make everything clearer," he whispered.

The entire canvas was my face. Eyes closed, and the rose rested behind my ear. All the black was my hair spread out, and the shades of gray were my face. The rose was so bright that your eyes just automatically focused on it. "It just became my favorite!" I exclaimed, excited. "Can you take it down to my room for me?" I asked him, then wondered if he was still feeling the effects of my medication. I reached out to him as his hand slipped away. "Wait. ... Don't. ... If something happens to it ..." I suddenly couldn't finish a complete sentence.

Grinning, Sorin gently picked up the painting. "My head is less hindered. Your painting will safely reach your room, don't fret."

He started to the door and stopped so I could lead. I took slow steps down to my room. I was still moving a little awkwardly. Sitting on my bed, I waited for him to enter. A moment later, he walked through the doorway, painting in hand. I looked around the room, trying to pick a place to have him hang it. The only things that hung up on my walls currently we're the candle sconces which were now used daily. I pointed to the wall near my side of the bed. Empty nails jutted from the walls where pictures of my family had once hung.

"Just lay it against the wall over here, and I will hang it later," I said, watching him move with fluid smoothness. He propped the painting against the wall and joined me on the bed. "So you feel better?" I asked quietly. He simply nodded a yes. "No more ... kissing for a while?" I asked, the disappointment clear in my voice. I felt like the past days had only increased my feelings for him. Every day, I was slowly learning more about him, seeing yet another side to him.

Sorin scowled. "You were very persistent throughout your life, I presume. No kissing, Mia." He sat back and crossed his arms over his chest. "We need to be careful. I have proved I cannot keep my wits about me when we … succumb to our desires." His eyes circled me. "I cannot hurt you again. … It could be more than a broken bone next time."

I rolled my eyes. "Hairline fracture. … I'll be fine in six to eight weeks. Sooner if you want to stop being stubborn."

Sorin leaned toward me. "Mia, you do not understand what you are asking of me." He ran his fingers through his hair, frustrated. "Are you willing to risk a permanent bond between us? Because the only thing that could torture me more than waiting for you to decide if a future with me is what you want … would be for us to unite and you to regret it. I've seen it happen. Anya was just one case of separation that I have witnessed personally. The more we exchange blood … even small amounts will affect us." He looked away. "I have tasted you, Mia. … Each time it makes me want you more. It makes you feel a pull to me. I am sure after our last encounter I can try to control myself, knowing I have hurt you. But I really should leave for a day. … It would be best. I could give you more time if I satisfied my appetite elsewhere."

I fell back onto the bed. "No!" I said loudly. "I understand it must sound bizarre to you that I think it such an intimate act. To you it's just food, but to me … the thought of you drinking someone's blood … it's just …" I swallowed and stared at the ceiling above me. "Don't go," I added. "I would rather risk my safety." I turned my head in his direction, waiting for him to agree not to go.

"Company," Sorin announced.

"What?" I said, puzzled.

"You have company, Mia." He nodded to the door.

I sat up just as the doorbell chimed. I made an irritated sound, ranting that everyone—no, the whole world—had poor timing. I moved to my dresser, and Sorin helped me slip into a pair of jeans. The doorbell sounded again, and I left the bedroom, shutting the door behind me. Hurrying down the stairs, my head was light from all the sudden movement. I flung the front door open, and sunlight poured in. I lifted my right hand over my eyes to shield them.

Natalie was walking back to her car. She held a plate of cookies in her hand. I called out to her, and she doubled back. Her smile faded as she approached the doorway. "Mia?" she asked with concern, looking at my sling.

"Oh, it's nothing ... I just fell."

She stepped inside, and I closed the door behind her. Natalie looked around at all the covered-up windows, and more lines filled her forehead. "Mia, honey, are you doing okay? The sisters were talking about how you weren't going to make it in for a few days. So we thought I should just stop in with some cookies and check up on you."

I looked upstairs, thinking it best to move the conversation to the kitchen. I gestured to her, and she led. I waited for her to put some distance between us. "Please stay upstairs," I said as quietly as I could.

Natalie turned and looked at me. "What was that, sweetie?"

I smiled. "The cookies look delicious," I said lightly as I caught up to her. She had just started working at the coffee shop with my mother and the twins shortly before the accident. I had only talked to her a handful of times. I felt like she was trying to win me over. My mother usually handled the bakery part of the shop; now Natalie was taking over the bakery duties. But I had no ill feelings toward her. We sat and talked for a while, and I made her tea. Her eyes always went to my sling or the side of my face that was bruised.

After stuffing myself with cookies, I politely said I needed to get back to work. I was pleased Sorin had listened to me or possibly stayed away on his own. I walked Natalie to the door and told her for the third time I was okay. Promising to come by the coffee shop soon, I thanked her for the visit. I shut the door behind her and walked to the farthest window, pushing the curtain aside a few inches. Just as I suspected, Natalie was digging through her purse and eventually pulled out her cell phone. I let the curtain fall back and moaned; I was minutes away from Jennifer calling. I cleaned up the kitchen, rinsing everything with one hand.

Chapter 5

I returned upstairs, where Sorin lay waiting for me. "Thanks," I said. "I think my appearance was enough for Natalie to worry about. A strange man in the house would have sent her over the edge."

He smiled. "You asked me to stay upstairs; I stayed. No need to explain your reasons." He patted the bed, and I circled to the other side of it, slipping in and curling up next to him. Lying silent for a few minutes, I finally said, "I should really go upstairs and work on my paintings." I turned on my side and could see Sorin thinking. His eyes looked heavy, like he was sleepy. "Are you tired?" I had not yet seen him sleep. "I'm going to the attic. Close your eyes and sleep awhile."

His eyes fluttered. "I should come up with you ... in case you need any assistance."

I could tell he was fighting it. I slipped from my side of the bed and walked to my dresser. I undid my pants and considered asking for help. But as I looked at the mirror in front of me, Sorin's reflection showed his eyes were already closed. So I quietly struggled to get out of them, leaving them on the floor. I started to creep past Sorin but stopped to watch him for a moment. He lay on top of the covers, which pleased me. My eyes fell on his lips, and I couldn't help but try to steal a kiss. As gently as I could, I lowered myself onto the bed next to him. I tested my possibility of success, reaching out and tracing his jawline down to his chin; there was no response. So I lowered my hand and leaned in, focusing on his mouth. Just as I was about to join my lips with his, the corner of one side of his mouth twitched and turned up a little. I sat up and sighed, disappointed. "I just wanted a kiss, just one." I could hear the disappointment in my own voice.

His mouth widened into a slight smile, but he kept his eyes closed. "I know," he said with confidence. "Just a kiss ... not wonderful deep metallic kisses." I waited for him to say no. "I know," he repeated. I sat quiet until I realized Sorin had yet to refuse me.

My stomach fluttered, and I leaned in and quickly kissed him. I pulled away briefly and kissed him again, a little longer the second time. Both were light and soft, nothing like the day before. I stood up and walked to the doorway, but I couldn't refrain from the question nagging me. "Why didn't you say no?" I asked.

He grinned, eyes still closed. "You had no intention of more than what you just did." He said it with such conviction. "The medication may be altering the colors I see around you, but not what I feel from you."

I felt there was nothing more to say, so I walked out of the room.

I spent a few hours in the attic sketching rough drafts on the empty canvases. It actually felt good to be painting again. Like I was reclaiming a part of myself. After a while, my wrist started aching, and I returned to the bedroom. Sorin sat up, looking quite refreshed.

"You've been here a week, and I have seen you sleep once."

His body stiffened a little. "Twice I have slept twice since being here with you. The first time I didn't exactly have a choice." The night I took the pill. I just stood there, not sure what to say. He reached over to the nightstand and picked up two pills and a glass of water for me to take.

I looked at the nightstand and then at my dresser. "You can give me the bottles. You don't need to worry about me." I accepted the pills and took them. Then I ate the banana he offered so I wouldn't upset my stomach. I had a lingering medicinal taste in my mouth, so I brushed my teeth before climbing into bed. I sat facing Sorin, trying to decide if I was hungry or not. His eyes made a wide circle around my body. "What do you have to say?" I said, unimpressed, feeling like I was constantly being evaluated.

He leaned over and tucked a few loose strands of hair behind my ear. "I think you look beautiful, Mia. Your colors are gradually improving every day. I feel hopeful. I no longer worry as I did when I first met you." He smiled. "But I will keep your wretched pills, just the same. I can see you are trying to return to your previous life; the past day alone was challenging, I'm sure." His eyes fell to the bed between us. "It has been a week since you buried your parents. Maybe a visit to them … or I could help you pack up their belongings. … Something to help you find closure." His eyes returned to mine, which began to water. "I feel you still fighting it, Mia. Accepting that your parents are gone. You need to mourn if you are going to regain a sense of living and stability." His voice was firm but gentle.

I stared off behind Sorin, knowing everything he said was true. Almost every time I awoke, for a brief moment, I forgot they were gone. Every day, I was careful not to touch anything that had belonged to my parents. I had not packed anything of theirs. There was still an empty teacup with a saucer and spoon sitting on the counter. My mother had forgotten to put it in the sink the morning of the accident. But every time I looked at it, I told myself she had just finished her morning tea and was off doing something in another room. It had become this bittersweet reminder. I was afraid to touch my father's clothes and smell his mint aftershave. I had gone through the motions the week before, but I had not truly said good-bye. As much pain as I knew it would cause, it was time to stop ignoring my loss. I simply tried not to think about it. But Sorin was right: it was time to mourn.

Tears fell down my cheek, and Sorin gently wiped them away. I looked at him and nodded in agreement. He moved closer, and I leaned into his shoulder softly crying. "I just need to take it slow; bear with me," I whispered. "Maybe you can help me pack some things tomorrow." He kissed my cheek and wrapped an arm around my right side.

My phone sounded, and I wasn't surprised when I saw Jennifer's phone number and name. The conversation went as expected. I lied and said I had fallen, hurting my wrist and bruising my cheek. I downplayed it all, promising to visit in a few days. I hung up and curled back up next to Sorin on the bed.

Over the next several days, I split my time between working on my paintings and packing up my parents' belongings. When it became too much, Sorin was always there to comfort me. He would walk me back to my room and hold me until the tears stopped. I pushed myself, and every day, he would look at me and say I was beautiful, that my colors were improving. I stopped taking the medication, choosing to feel everything, emotionally and physically. I was eating regularly again and spending at least an hour or two outside in the sun. Between gaining a few pounds and getting fresh air daily, I slowly felt more myself again. Color was back in my cheeks, and my skin had tanned. Sorin helped me with anything that was too difficult because of my arm—with the exception of bathing. It was a struggle, but I managed without his assistance. The clock was returned to the kitchen wall. We shared a few soft kisses but nothing more. I was content curling up next to him daily in bed. I asked very few personal questions of him, sticking instead to his interests. In return, Sorin never brought up my intentions for the future.

I had promised the mama bears I would visit, and it was now days overdue. My bruises had faded some, and acquiring a tan helped my appearance. I could no longer put it off. I went to my closet, hoping that maybe if I dressed up and put some makeup on, it would distract from my injured wrist. I chose a dress that my mother had bought me earlier that spring. Bright and floral, something I would never wear. But the print was a guaranteed diversion. I took it off the hanger and laid it on the bed. It fell just above my knees and had crossing straps over the back. It was a large print of hydrangeas, blues and lavender on a cream background. It had rained the day before and cooled slightly. I thought it wouldn't hurt to grab a short-sleeved cardigan that buttoned down the front, covering my sling. I could picture the sweater, just couldn't remember where I'd put it last. I flipped through the clothes on the hangers, looking for the cream color, but found nothing. I looked to the overhead shelf, and the box from Paris sat there, just above my head. I wanted to know what was in it, but I trusted Sorin to give it to me when he thought best. I shut the closet door, giving up on finding the cardigan. I slipped into the dress easily, getting my injured arm through the spaghetti straps, and then I removed the tag. But without being able to use both hands, I couldn't zip up the back.

I called for Sorin, who had excused himself when I headed to the shower earlier. He slowly entered, and I turned to my dresser, searching for a comb. "I need help with the zipper in back … do you mind?" I had so many things racing through my head, I didn't bother waiting for a response. I picked up the bottle of scented oil he had sent for, and put some on my good wrist and the sling.

I felt his fingers pinch the base of the zipper, and I stilled my movements so he could lift it with ease. My eyes continued to looking around my dresser for the comb. I waited, feeling Sorin's right hand trace my spine. His fingertips began at the base and slowly crept upward. There was instant electricity, and I trembled at his touch on my exposed back. My eyes darted to the mirror in front of me as I clung to the dresser with my right hand. My heart began to race. His eyes only saw the skin his fingers traced. He hadn't touched me like this since I had been hurt almost a week before. I knew if my room had been lit by the usual candles I would see a reflection of fiery purple. His fingers retraced their path to the zipper below. Sorin's sight never wavered from my skin.

"Sorin?" I finally breathed. It was enough to snap him out of the moment. He lifted the zipper quickly, kissed my bare shoulder, and turned to leave. I spun to face him. "Sorin?" I repeated, confused.

He kept his back to me as he stood in the doorway. "I am sorry, Mia … I can no longer put off satisfying my hunger. I will leave tonight once the sun is down." He said it with regret, knowing how I felt about it. I was beginning to believe he had put it off this long only for me. He walked away, leaving the door open behind him.

My head screamed to go after him and convince him to wait just another night or two. I combed my wet hair, leaving it down. I put on some purple eye shadow and pink lipstick. Again, something colorful to draw attention away from my injury. I didn't see Sorin as I came downstairs, but I worried little, as it was midday and very sunny. I had hours to persuade him to hold off a little longer.

I visited the coffee shop, just as I had promised the mama bears I would. Jennifer fussed over my arm resting in its sling. Thankfully, she hadn't seen me the day after Sorin's and my intimate encounter had gone so wrong. Gina reached out and brushed my hair back from my shoulder, commenting on not having seen it down in so long. I lifted the sling lightly, joking about my wrist influencing my daily hairstyle. They asked if I needed anything, and I politely assured them I didn't. The afternoon rush began, and I accepted hugs before leaving, promising I would return after my painting obligation to James from the pizzeria was fulfilled.

I took the plate of baked goods they gave me, eating some on the way home. I set the plate of pastries on the kitchen counter when I entered the house, and then I went upstairs to change. I thought of everything I could say to get Sorin to postpone leaving me. I knew sooner or later he would reach a breaking point if he continued abstaining. I honestly did not know what the result would be if I kept pushing him.

Accepting his lifestyle as my own, however, was something I still struggled with deeply. My feelings for Sorin were strong. I just feared they were due to the timing when he entered my life for the second time. My only option was to let him go out to feed. I headed upstairs, heavyhearted. Realizing the shower was running as I entered my room, I slowed my movements, stepping out of my sandals. I undid the sling and let it drop to the floor. I lit the few closest candles and shut off the light. Maybe talking to him would keep him here just one more night.

The bathroom door opened, and Sorin stepped out. He wore a pair of ebony pajama bottoms of a thin material, and they rested below his waist. I slowly noticed more. He still had water droplets on his body, and his hair was tousled. Shivers spread throughout my body as my desire to touch his bare skin intensified. My eyes followed the curve of his muscles, and I noticed how tense he was. His jaw was tight, and his hands wrung the towel they held. My pulse raced when I looked into his eyes. They were a bright metallic purple, and I rushed to him. I threw my right arm around him, grabbing the back of his neck. I lowered his face and pressed my lips into his. I was aggressive, forceful, and when he tried to pull away I only tightened my grip. I parted my lips, teasing his with mine.

"Kiss me, Sorin," I rasped against his face, aching for his touch. "Touch me," I begged.

He pulled his head away easily, despite my fingers trying to hold him near. "I should go, Mia. I need to be far away from you right now." His voice was worried, frustrated.

My head was light, and I enjoyed the rush of blood throughout my body. "It's daylight, Sorin. ... You can't run away," I said quietly, optimism filling me.

He was trapped inside the house for hours—with me.

I guided him to the edge of the bed. He sat with his hands on either side of him, his body rigid. I pictured him trying to lock himself away in the attic or guest room until nightfall, and I almost teased him about having no options. But, saying nothing, I closed the gap between us and reached out to cup his face. His hand shot up, stopping mine; I knew not to struggle.

"Just a kiss," I pleaded. He looked up at me as I stood over him. His eyes circled my face, and he quickly turned away.

"Mia ... a blind man could see your intentions right now." His voice was low.

"So let me start with a kiss." I lightly kissed his cheek and then lowered to his neck in a soft trail. The towel he held fell to the floor. Sorin's body shook lightly, which encouraged me further. I pressed myself against him, and we fell back onto the bed. My hurt arm rested on his chest, and he laid his hand over it. "Kiss me, Sorin," I said as seductively as I could. Violet eyes met mine, and the fiery purple burned into me. His free hand cupped my face delicately and lowered it to his.

After a few slow, controlled kisses, I could no longer restrain myself. Parting his lips with mine, I slid my tongue over his teeth. A disappointed sigh escaped me. "I want to feel them," I purred, not sure how to make him respond.

"Mia!" he said through clenched teeth.

"Please, Sorin," I whispered while lightly kissing him.

As I dug my nails into his chest, his body tensed below me, and then his kisses turned bold. A deep growl sounded in his chest as he drew my bottom lip between his teeth, piercing into it with his fangs. A light sound of shock sounded in my head, but I didn't pull away. He nursed my lip, lightly shuddering repeatedly. I moaned, starting to feel light-headed. He abruptly let go, forcing me away.

"No!" I complained, licking my lips, the taste of my blood subtle. "More!" I urged, trying to press against him again.

"Mia?" He sounded hesitant.

"I want to taste you now," I said, breathless. "I understand there is a dangerous cliff that I may overstep the edge of as a result of kissing you like this." I took a deep breath. "My intention is to not reach that point of no return. But I know that fall could happen at any moment … and I do not fear the fall, knowing you will be the one to catch me."

His right hand entangled in my hair, just above my neck, and lowered my face to his. Sorin kissed me briefly, and then he turned his attention to his wrist near my face. His fingers stayed entwined in my hair, but he repositioned his face between mine and his wrist.

I couldn't see anything, as his face rested against mine. But I felt a slight movement in his facial muscles. Sorin's lips returned to mine, brushing them. Instantly they tingled, and I licked them, tasting his blood. The tip of my tongue quickly felt the same tingling. Eager and nervous, I opened my mouth over his. Another frustrated sound rumbled through him as he hesitated.

"Please, Sorin," I said after a moment.

He gently rolled me to my back and sealed his lips over mine. His blood slowly seeped into my mouth, exploding. It tasted like a candy I had loved as a child. A million tiny explosions filled my mouth. I opened my eyes in surprise, thrilled at the sensation. I swallowed, and the explosions flowed down my throat. Sorin lifted his face from mine, and I gasped for air. His eyes looked into mine, and then they lowered to my neck, fluttering. His mouth was closed tightly, and I realized why.

"Again," I sweetly demanded.

He obeyed, closing his eyes and kissing me. The metallic liquid filled me, and my body reacted the same way as it had before. I quietly squealed in response.

After a few minutes, the explosions dissipated, and Sorin moved away as I opened my eyes. I lightly smiled and slipped my arm around his waist in an attempt to pull him close. He unexpectedly moved farther away. A moment later, he stood near the doorway.

"That is enough, Mia. … We should stop." He sounded upset.

I sat up, slid off the bed, and stood before him. He looked tense, anxious, and I thought he would walk out the door. Caught up in the moment, I reached around and unzipped my dress without a second thought. It fell to the floor around my feet. I stepped out of it, walking toward Sorin.

"I don't want to stop," I said, with all the confidence I could muster. I walked to his side, a little self-conscious that all I wore was a pair of underwear. I placed my hand on his shoulder and kissed his neck lightly. "Come to bed." I looked into his eyes and dropped my hand to his. I stepped back and tried to guide him to the bed.

His arm lifted between us, but his feet didn't budge. "Mia," Sorin said, shaking his head, "you cannot be suggesting ... I broke your wrist while only kissing you." The purple quickly left his eyes.

I wanted to feel him against me, no clothing between us. Feel him touch me. "I may not know what I want tomorrow ... but I know what I want tonight."

He looked away. "I do not wish to upset you ... but my desire for you in my future far outweighs any other I currently feel." His eyes drifted over the bed. "We have already done too much, I fear."

I let go of his hand and sat on the bed, pulling the sheet to cover myself. "Sorin, look at me." He did as I asked. "We are at an impasse. You need something tonight ... something I can give you." I paused, sighing. "And I need something ... you. I am sure we can figure something out. You try to be gentle, and I won't panic and twist any limbs away." I lightly smiled. Deep inside I knew what I was risking.

"It is impossible, Mia! I am saying this because it has happened. I have heard the horror stories. Seen the guilt and disgust on the faces of those who accidentally injured someone while intimate." He crossed his arms.

My mouth moistened a little, and the bitter taste began. I flicked my tongue over the roof of my mouth to confirm it. "You are lying," I snapped, insulted he would even try to lie right to my face.

He looked confused, and his back tensed up. "What?" he said, clearly puzzled.

"You are telling me that there is no way we could be intimate the way I want to … unless I'm like you. But it is a lie, I can taste it." I didn't understand why he was doing this.

He repeated, "It is not possible. I could guarantee your getting hurt."

I tasted the bitterness even more strongly. "Why are you lying to me, Sorin?" I said, hurt. I suddenly recalled something he had said earlier. Maybe Sorin didn't actually believe he was lying to me. "Is there something you are not saying?" I pressed. "You believe it possible somehow." I waited. I could see him thinking about it before explaining.

"There is something … but it would not be possible for us. I am beginning to wish it was an option."

I was intrigued. "Explain it to me, please."

Sorin crossed to the wall near the bathroom and leaned against it. His eyes returned to their usual silvery ice blue as the candles caught them. "When a bond is formed between two vampires … once united, they feel what the other feels. It begins emotionally, eventually becomes physical, and on rare occasions, a mental bond is formed. After repeating the exchange of blood over such a long period of time, a couple can sometimes … share one another's thoughts visually. But it is extremely rare, and we have not completed a bond. You have not turned yet … you don't even know if you want that life." He began to pace slowly, clearly uncomfortable.

I smiled lightly, remembering the time in the kitchen and imagining Sorin crossing to me. A second time, when he was on the phone with Monique, I had a similar vision. They were both intense but had a dreamlike feel to them. I started to feel elated at the prospect. My heart began to race as I relived the dreamlike moments with Sorin.

He stopped pacing and turned to me quickly. His eyes made a circle around me, and he began shaking his head. "It is possible … I think it has already happened." I patted the bed next to me. "I think it is wishful thinking. … It is abnormal that we feel as much as we do now, considering we have not united."

I couldn't decipher whether he didn't believe me or just did not want it to be true. "Well, you just said we are already very in tune with one another. More than we should be. Maybe we are an exception to the rule. No part of our past is the norm, correct?" My smile deepened. Slipping from bed, I let the sheet fall away from me. "I just want to try."

Sorin's eyes turned to the floor. "Under one condition, Mia." His voice was displeased.

I wrinkled my nose, wondering what it would be. Reluctantly, I agreed. "Fine, what is the stipulation?"

"Please cover yourself … so I can concentrate." His tone had changed, as if he had been defeated.

I happily moved to my dresser and pulled out an emerald-green camisole. As I moved my arm through the spaghetti strap gingerly, I realized it wasn't as tender. I figured being focused on other things caused the usual pain to seem less. I shrugged and turned my attention back to Sorin. "Better?" I smiled, starting to feel butterflies.

He forced a smile and nodded.

I quickly moved to the bed. "Now what?" Impatient, I reached out for him. He circled around and sat at the head of the bed with his back to the wall. I turned around to face him. He let his legs part, crossing them at the ankles. I moved closer to him and mimicked his position. I crossed my ankles and let my knees fall outward. He reached out on either side and untied the canopy curtains. Sorin weakly smiled and laid his hands on the bed, palms down and near his thighs.

"I can behave myself," I fussed, not wanting to follow his example.

His smile faded, and he looked down at my hands resting in my lap. I frowned and tucked my right hand under my leg. He sighed and leaned forward to kiss me, and I matched his movement. He kissed me softly, and I moaned at the tenderness. I moved away, ready to experience what I had before.

"Now what?" I asked. His eyes were still silvery ice blue, and disappointment washed over me.

"Kiss me again, Mia," he said flatly.

We kissed again, only this time he gently bit my lip, drawing blood out for a minute. As before, it was nothing more than a slight pinching sensation. He released my lip and proceeded to bite himself. The tiny explosions began, and my heart raced as I tried to continue sitting on my hand.

A deep moan escaped Sorin, and I opened my eyes, seeing the fiery purple I had been waiting for. He kept his face close but stopped kissing me. "Now close your eyes." His voice was silken, hypnotic. I fought it; I wanted to look into his eyes. "Close your eyes, and just listen to my voice," he said.

The warm snowflakes began to fall, and my eyelids grew heavy. I closed them.

"Now clear your mind of everything, just picture black everywhere." His voice caressed me, and I filled my mind with darkness. "Now picture clouds; you're outside, and all you see is a sky full of clouds as you look up at it above you." Again, I did as he asked. He continued describing everything he saw.

Sorin stood before me, shirtless in his ebony pajama bottoms. I knew this was in my head because sunlight touched his skin. I looked around a circle of weeping willows that surrounded us. We were in a botanical garden full of flowers, all in bloom. I was speechless. The colors were a composition of blues and purples. Irises, roses, and tall hydrangeas. Some of the flowers I had never seen before, and I wondered if they were things Sorin had seen or just created. Beautiful lavender and light-blue morning glories twisted themselves around the tree trunk, spreading out a cover of blossoms over most of the ground around us. The sun was bright but not blinding; the temperature perfect. There was a slight breeze that held a floral scent.

Looking down, I realized I wore a bright-yellow dress made of light gauze. It wrapped tightly around me and ended just above the knees. I made a repulsed sound at the color and style choice, looking up at Sorin.

"Change it," he said, softly smiling.

I imagined a dress of another color and a slightly different style. As I looked down, the yellow seemed to bleed from the fabric. Slowly from the top, a deep purple began, lowering to the bottom of the dress. As the new color reached the bottom, the fabric lengthened. Now a deep-purple dress of light silk ending just above my ankles moved softly in the breeze. I giggled quietly, in awe. "This is amazing ... unreal," I finally said out loud.

Sorin continued to smile. "It is real in your mind." He reached out and took my left hand, kissing it. I realized it felt just fine.

Moving closer to him, I tilted my head up for a kiss. Something tickled my shoulder, and I stepped back. A butterfly flew off, and I gasped softly. Bright vivid butterflies swirled around us, in colors that matched the flowers. "Everything is incredible, Sorin." I looked down at the lush grass that tickled my bare feet. "But ..." I said, my voice low.

He lifted my face to his, and a light kiss followed. "What is it?" His voice was seductive.

"It is all so beautiful ... but too much." I looked up at the butterflies dancing around us, and they flew off into the trees. As I looked higher to the sun, it became a full moon, overly large in the sky and pouring out its silvery light. I looked around one more time. "And something is missing."

Sorin stepped back to survey our surroundings. Puzzled, he turned back to me.

I pictured a small white gazebo on the edge of the garden around us, and it began to appear. He took my hand, leading me to it.

As we reached the few steps before the entrance, he swiftly scooped me up. I slid my arms around his neck and rested my head on his shoulder. He stopped on the last step, and I lifted my head, concerned that even under these circumstances Sorin was still hesitant. Quickly a canopy of sheer fabric matching my dress poured out from the center of the ceiling. It draped down to the lower frame of the gazebo. The sheer fabric only slightly darkened the inside of the gazebo. I wasn't sure if it was meant for privacy or intended to simulate my bed. It was thoughtful, either way. He stepped inside and carried me to the center. We both looked down at the wooden flooring.

Just as I attempted to imagine hundreds of pillows, I was greeted by a soft floor. Looking down, a single oversized pillow covered the gazebo floor. Light lavender satin lay against my exposed skin, and a few small pillows supported my head. Sorin eased me back onto them and sat to my left, our hips touching. Everything was perfect. The scent of flowers in the air, the moonlight, and a sense that we were the only two people in the world.

I couldn't help but wonder aloud. "How many times have you done this?" I whispered, trying not to let images of Sorin intimate with another woman in this way fill my head. Even if this was only in our minds, it felt real.

He gently picked up my left hand, laying it against his face, and kissed my wrist. A small smile appeared on his lips. "This is my first time, Mia. ... It is possible only through a blood bond. That is why I had my doubts." He let go of my hand and leaned in to kiss me.

I unexpectedly felt a surge of anxiety rush through me. Sorin paused and moved back to a sitting position. His eyes circled me, and lines creased his forehead. I knew he would ask, so I spoke up. "This is my first time ... like this, obviously ... and I know it's all in my head. But it has been a really long time since I ..." My words trailed off, and I felt embarrassed. I looked away, not knowing how to explain what I was feeling.

Sorin lifted my chin, turning my face in his direction, and his ice-blue eyes entranced me. "Nothing will happen that you do not want to. You are safe in your room, in your bed, and you can open your eyes to end this whenever you wish." His tone was low, comforting. "We can stay here as long as you want." His words soothed me, and I relaxed into the pillows around me.

Sorin's left arm crossed over my body, resting on the pillow as he leaned over me. I reached up and cupped his face, lowering it to me and kissing him. It all felt different this time, maybe because I felt like I was usually the aggressor. I was the one surrendering this time. Gradually his kisses deepened, and I sighed with pleasure. My eyes closed as he took my hand, pressing it to his chest. Sorin's heart pounded beneath my palm, and I loved it.

After a few minutes, our hands left his chest and rested above my head. The pillow below me moved as he changed his position. His fingers delicately moved the dress strap off my shoulder and traced the curve of my neck. His kisses softened again, as his hand left my neck, easing past my chest to my side. I arched my body, ready for his touch. Sorin's hand lowered even farther, exploring my body. His hand squeezed my hip before continuing. At my ankle, he grabbed a handful of fabric and raised it slowly to my knees. My heart raced as the anticipation grew. He repeated the motion, lifting more fabric to my upper thigh. Air touched my now bare legs as the hem of my dress rested above my knees. Sorin moved his hand to my exposed knee, and then he paused. I moaned in urgency against his kisses, feeling him smile lightly. His touch lifted to my inner thigh as he moved his hand away from my knee.

At last, his hand found its destination, and I gasped. Instantly, chills shot through my body. Turning my head away suddenly, trying to catch my breath, I squeezed my eyes shut. His fingers began their tender massage, and I covered my mouth, muffling my tortured cries.

His lips grazed my ear. "Do you want me to stop, Mia?" His voice made my head light.

I considered opening my eyes and ending it all, suddenly nervous. My body was quickly responding to his touch. I feared it wouldn't be long before his efforts achieved their desired effect. My mind screamed to stop, to save myself from an embarrassing outcome. But my body ached for his touch to increase its pace. I reached out, grabbing at the pillow below me. I shook my head and began to move against him.

"Sorin," I said, quietly begging him to continue. He planted soft kisses on my neck and shoulder. His motions gradually increased, and I mirrored them.

Within a few minutes, I was staring at my bedroom ceiling as I lay shuddering. Slowly, dancing shadows of roses came into focus. I lay still for a moment, my heart racing, my cheeks flushed, completely content. I had forgotten how wonderful what I had just experienced felt. The blissful fog started to lift, and I sat up abruptly, beginning to feel a little embarrassed.

Sorin hadn't moved at all. His hands still rested at his sides. He looked completely relaxed, a small smile on his lips and an expression of admiration. But he was looking at me as if it were the first time he laid eyes on me. I could see Sorin's silvery-blue eyes studying every inch of me. My heartbeat returned to normal, and I sat silent.

"Mia, you are absolutely gorgeous right now." His voice was warm and soft.

"What colors do you see right now? Try to describe them to me." I placed my hands in my lap and waited, interested.

He leaned back against the wall. "Anything I say would not do you justice. … There are no words for the beauty I see before me."

I could feel his words fall onto my skin. Warm snowflakes slowly melting all over my body. "Try," I said quietly, wanting to have some idea of the image he saw.

"Gold … bright tiny specks of gold encircling you and on your skin. I have never seen this color before. The gold color swiftly fading away as time passes." He paused, and his smile left. "I will certainly miss you surrounded by such a breathtaking sight." He sounded disappointed.

Any lingering feelings of contentment dissolved as I realized what his words meant. "I have not agreed yet, Sorin. … I still have my reservations." I said it slowly, hoping he understood I meant it. Every day with him only made me want him more. I had begun to crave a future with Sorin, wishing to leave this life behind me. Only I had to let go completely and accept that it was truly what I wanted. I had no desire to have this conversation right now. My thoughts returned to the lush and colorful botanical garden. "Everything was so vivid and seemed so real." I smiled, reminiscing.

Sorin sighed, and a grin tugged at the corner of his mouth. "Real enough," he lovingly teased.

I blushed, apologizing. "I'm sorry," I whispered, looking away.

He reached out and turned my face back to his. "You have no reason to apologize." He looked at my lips before a short kiss.

I shifted, uncomfortable. "But it ended before you could … I didn't mean to open my eyes and end it so suddenly." I bit at my lip, not wanting to admit it. "It has been a long time since …" I couldn't say the words aloud.

He kissed me again and held the side of my face. "It was a beautiful ending," he said affectionately. He kissed me again, only longer this time.

"But aren't you a little … unsatisfied?" I finally braved the question I had been wondering.

He looked deep into my eyes as he spoke. "You forget; I feel what you feel, Mia … maybe not as intense. But pleasure and release, just the same."

His eyes drifted to my neck, and their color darkened from the silvery ice blue to a light violet.

Brushing my hair back from my neck, I tilted my head to the side, exposing as much skin as I could. "You satisfied my appetite. … It is only fair I satisfy yours." My pulse increased its rate as I pictured Sorin gathering me into his arms.

His eyes intensified to a deep purple.

I moved closer and leaned on my left hand.

He looked down at my hand and then back to me. "You still haven't noticed." His voice was touched with disappointment.

I quickly lifted my hand and rolled my wrist a few times, instantly smiling. "It doesn't hurt at all," I said, pleased, wondering exactly when the lingering pain had finally stopped. I lightly touched the place that held the bruises from Sorin's first bite weeks before.

I leaned forward and kissed him. I put both of my palms against his bare chest. As the kisses deepened, so did my nails. Sorin sucked in a sharp breath against my mouth, and I moved away.

"Sorry, I didn't mean to …" I let my voice trail off as I took a deep breath, sitting up and looking down at my left wrist one more time before lifting it to him.

"Mia?" Sorin asked, unsure.

"Kiss it," I urged softly. "Like you did our first evening together."

He reached out and cradled my wrist. I pressed it against his mouth gently. "Kiss it," I repeated. I felt a tinge of nervousness and swallowed hard.

His eyes looked to my wrist as he kissed it delicately. Inhaling, Sorin parted his lips, pausing briefly before piercing my skin. My body only slightly tensed as I felt the pressure increase. A low quiet gasp escaped me. My heart raced as his eyes locked with mine. He continued filling himself with my blood, moving very little. My head began to feel light and dizzy. Sorin's eyes glazed over, and he was no longer focused on me. His hand tightened around my wrist, and I instantly knew he was lost.

Taking a deep breath, I told myself to stay calm, not pull away like last time. I just had to gain his attention and save myself from what I knew was imminent. My head spun, and my eyes grew heavy as my vision blurred. It was too late. I exhaled, embracing the darkness that was waiting to engulf me. I think Sorin's name left my lips before I lost consciousness.

It seemed as though a whole night had passed before I heard his voice off somewhere calling to me. "Mia … Mia, *amore*. Please open your eyes." His voice held a deep concern. The way he said my name.

Calling me his love brought me back. I smiled while still in darkness. I fought to open my eyes and watch him repeat himself. "Say it again," I finally whispered, opening my eyes.

He reached out and brushed my cheek. His eyes were a dark sapphire. I lay on my back in the center of the bed. A look of relief covered his face as he kissed my forehead. "I am truly sorry … I did not intend for that experience to end as it did Mia, *amore*."

I smiled, content. "It was a beautiful ending." I echoed his words from earlier.

He scowled and caressed my cheek again. Sorin moved from the bed and stopped at the doorway. "I will return with some food."

Chapter 6

He was gone only long enough for me to gather my thoughts and return to my side of the bed. Entering my room, he circled to my side of the bed, carrying a tray of food and a tall glass of juice. He had donned a shirt before returning to my room. Resting the tray full of food over my lap, he said, "You need to eat and gain your strength back." A guilty look crept over his expression. "I should not have taken so much from you."

Our eyes locked, as his tone meant more than my blood. I looked down at the plate of food before me, heavyhearted and too weak to argue. He moved around the room as I ate. First he sat near me, and then he circled the room. He sat on his side of the bed briefly, but quickly began to pace around the room, watching me eat. I had eaten most of my meal by then, and half the juice was gone.

"Sorin," I said, my voice unexpectedly loud. I paused and spoke more softly. "I'm all right. I feel perfectly fine. Don't worry, and stop pacing; you are making me dizzy. Why don't we go outside and get some fresh air?"

I started to move the tray from my lap. But he was at my side, removing it before I had lifted it an inch off the bed. I thanked him. He offered his arm to assist me off the bed, but I pushed it away. "I'm okay, really," I said.

It was only a mild lie. My legs felt shaky and, my head was still light. I moved to my dresser and put on something suitable for the backyard. Sorin waited in the doorway, his back to me as I dressed. I joined him, and he wrapped an arm around my waist protectively. I leaned against him as we descended the stairs, my legs unsteady beneath me.

The sun had just gone down, and it wasn't completely dark outside. I gently crumpled into a patio chair, relaxing. "Thank you," I said quietly, looking up at Sorin.

"For what?" he asked, unsure.

I was beginning to feel very comfortable emotionally with Sorin, able to reveal anything I was feeling. "Thank you for not leaving me tonight. For respecting how I feel about someone else being who you turn to for your needs."

His face was blank, and I thought maybe I had misunderstood. "I offered myself … you're not leaving now, right?" I could hear the panic in my own voice.

He leaned over and kissed the top of my head. "Mia … I feel that I have changed the course of your intended life. I deceived you when we met, and I have asked so much of you. It amazes me that you do not hate me for the things I have done." He leaned down and kissed me softly. "I would do everything I could to avoid deliberately causing you pain. I did not mean for you to greet darkness earlier. I realize now postponing feeding only increased the possibility of your being hurt. I should have stopped myself, been aware of how your body was responding." He began to walk away but turned back before stepping off the patio. "If you want me to shun all others and only drink from you at this time … I will happily obey your request. But remember what will result from honoring your wish." He said it bittersweetly and then turned to the yard ahead of him.

Sorin purposely left me to think about his words, and he sat on the grass twenty feet in front of me.

I looked down at my wrist where he had pierced the skin just hours before. My fingers traced over the circular bruises. I closed my eyes and lay my head back against the chair. It was impossible not to think about what I was asking him to do. It consumed me: If he did as I asked, it would only reinforce our bond. He had given me his blood, a part of him entrusting me. Sorin had knowingly made himself vulnerable, and I had done the same, with little regard. I thought of the words he had just left me with. They were reminiscent of marriage vows. I knew accepting his life as my own would tie us together forever. It was beyond marriage; no option for divorce. We were already a part of one another. My blood was currently flowing through him, and Sorin had been a part of me for years now. My fingers touched my lips as I thought of the taste of his blood. I was beginning to want a forever with him.

A little girl's squeal tore me from my thoughts. The neighbor girl, Scarlett, was running around her backyard, chasing fireflies. She was five or six and had strawberry blonde hair with bangs. Freckles covered her face and shoulders. She wore a pale-pink nightgown, which she tried not to trip over as she jumped around. Her family had moved in less than a month ago. I had been out on the back patio when the moving truck came. While her parents were otherwise occupied with the movers, she came into my yard and introduced herself so politely. She stayed and talked for a half hour. Only a few minutes of it had passed with her quietly watching me draw the tree line in the distance. The rest of it was her telling me all about herself: she had the same name as her grandmother, she was starting kindergarten in the fall, she wanted a puppy for

Christmas, she loved the color of her new bedroom—and on and on to everything in between. I was somewhat relieved when her parents finally retrieved her; I had begun to worry it would never end.

I looked closer now, seeing she had a firefly in her sights and watching her chase it all the way to my yard. She would run a few steps, then stop and jump, grabbing at the flicker of light. Scarlett slowly made her way near Sorin, and I sat up, interested. She squealed and giggled. I could see the firefly light just above his head as he turned to her. Scarlett only looked up, about to collide with Sorin. I leaned forward in my chair, a light feeling of suspense beginning to fill me. He was watching her, aware of her playful path. At the last minute, Sorin's body turned in her direction, and he caught her as she tripped. In one fluid movement, he stood her upright and trapped the firefly she had been chasing. He held his hand out to Scarlett. She leaned over it curious. Sorin slowly opened his hand and she giggled, happy at what she saw. She reached out for the tiny light he held, but it escaped. Scarlett looked sad, and her shoulders fell. I overheard her say she was too slow.

Sorin looked behind him and then over the little girl's head. He whispered something to her, and she nodded a yes in response. He gracefully stood and tapped the tip of her nose. She smiled, and Sorin became a blur throughout the yard. In less time than it took to draw a breath, he knelt before her, opening both hands. Two fistfuls of fireflies lit the space around the two of them as the tiny creatures escaped their prison. Scarlett squealed in delight, another high-pitched exclamation filling the air. She clapped and started jumping after them.

Sorin sat on the ground, facing me this time. My heart felt as if it were about to burst. I thought it was all so touching, but the feelings overcoming me I suspected we're not mine. Watching only Scarlett, Sorin smiled. Not the usual grin or soft smile I had seen before. But he laughed at her excitement, body lightly shaking as he flashed a perfect smile. Scarlett jumped over and over, and his smile grew even broader. He looked so normal in that moment, and I didn't want it to end.

Sorin's head quickly turned to the house next door, and he was instantly on his feet. He shooed Scarlett back to her yard, explaining her mother was looking for her. The whole scene had played out in a matter of minutes. Her mother opened the back door just as Scarlett stepped onto the back steps. I heard a light scolding for leaving the house without asking first. By the time I looked back to Sorin he was only a few feet from me.

He turned a chair toward me and sat down. "Mia … can you answer something for me?" He looked serious. His tone held a slight reluctance to it.

Whatever he was about to say, I knew he thought the conversation was overdue. I shrugged. "I can't lie to you … even if I wanted to." I sat back and tried to prepare myself.

He looked past me, his eyes settling on Scarlett's house, and then he looked at me again. "Do you desire to have a child?" His eyes held a deep sadness as he asked.

I was an only child, and my family lived so far from the few relatives we had. I had very little exposure to children. I sighed, not sure what he wanted me to say and not exactly sure how I felt. "I assume that means it will not to be an option if I choose a life with you." I understood most of the internal differences between human and vampire bodies, and presumed procreation was one of those things only human bodies could do.

Sorin frowned, and a few wrinkles appeared on his brow. "Did you intend on having children someday?" he asked.

I thought about it some more, pictured myself alone with him in our botanical garden. Then I closed my eyes and imagined myself with a husband, two children at a picnic in the park. I opened my eyes and weakly smiled. "I haven't given it a whole lot of thought these past few years. I think if children were not part of my future … I would accept it." The truth was, in this moment, Sorin was everything I wanted and hadn't even known was possible.

"It will no longer be an option if you choose a future with me, Mia. Be sure before you make your final decision," he said as he sat back in his chair.

I thought of his interaction with Scarlett. The way he smiled, enjoying her amusement. Something about it nagged at me. "Did you have children, Sorin?" I saw his face drain of any emotion. "In your previous life … did you have a wife and child?" A part of me already knew the answer.

Sorin's body eased deeper into his chair as his eyes looked off somewhere over my shoulder. He was recalling his other life. "We conceived twice. The first child was lost to us just after learning about his or her existence. The second I had felt kick within her for the first time a week before she fell ill." His expression stayed vacant, and I could see so many memories flood his sight. "It was an arranged marriage. We were so young, but we loved each other, surprisingly happy with the match and the future we would have together. All Mariana wanted was to be a mother. She talked about children all the time. She was overjoyed and then quickly heartbroken with the first child. With the second, she had finally allowed herself to revel in motherhood."

Sorin stopped, and his eyes fell lower but continued to focus elsewhere. "Mariana developed a terrible cough at the end of our second year together." His voice lowered. "I am sure had it been present day, some simple antibiotics would have saved them." Finally he looked at me. "I wondered for a long time what it would have been like ... to be a father. Create something that is a part of you. Watch it grow and go out into the world." He sighed. "But I have had many years to wonder what could have been."

I shifted in my chair and pondered it a little further. "I have never been married or had a child, and I have never daydreamed about what it would be like. I think the possibility of motherhood ending is an acceptable sacrifice. How could I truly long for or miss something I never possessed?" I said it delicately, all the while having faith in what I said. How could I regret turning away from something that had yet to exist?

Sorin leaned forward in his chair, an odd look on his face. "Do you think it unbelievable to long for someone you have never met? To know a part of you flows through another, while a sense of being incomplete overwhelms you daily?" He spoke just above a whisper, his voice causing my heart to ache as I understood he was no longer referring to his human life. A gentle wave of emotions flowed through me, and I knew they were not my own. It was a mixture of loneliness and frustration. My chest seemed to tighten in response.

I found the courage to ask him what I had wondered so many times before. "What was it like these past twenty-four years, Sorin?" He had talked about it in passing comments. Explaining the pull he had felt over the years. He always seemed to be holding back, or stopping, just as he was about to reveal something.

Sorin's eyes drifted off, unfocused on anything. Clearly thinking of those years, he shivered. After a moment, he looked at me. "Do you really want to know, Mia?" His voice was soft but begged me to say yes.

I suddenly wondered about how awful it must have been. All I did was nod, hoping I wouldn't regret it.

He sat back and crossed his arms over his chest. "After seeing for myself how much your father and mother loved one another, I knew she would never willingly leave him. The way they looked at each other. To witness your father touching your mother's expanding abdomen and talking about fatherhood." He raked his fingers through his hair. My chest tightened further, and Sorin laid a hand on his own chest briefly.

"It was you and Mariana all over again," I said, my voice cracking as tears threatened.

He sorrowfully agreed and pressed on. "I could not allow myself to destroy such a beautiful union. But I could not stay near your mother and ignore my desire to claim her." His body relaxed a little into the chair as the sensation in my chest lessened. "Only when you want free will can you find it. I left. ... I had to, and it took my going across the ocean to feel any sense of relief. The first year was the hardest. It is an obsession, almost madness that overcomes you. The same thoughts repeat in your mind: *Embrace her. ... Claim her. ... Possess her. ... Only then will you be a complete again.*" My eyes widened at such mental torment. "I sought out the one who embraced me into this existence. With his help, your mother continued the life she clearly loved."

Sorin sighed, and I waited, feeling his heartbreak as my own. A yearning to share more, but giving me a chance to end it here. It was a pain he longed to share, to finally free himself of. Maybe hearing it all would aid me in understanding him more. "What did you do?" I asked quietly.

The lighting had changed; moonlight now filled the backyard. As his head tilted a certain way, I could see his eyes were now dark sapphire. His voice became tense. "I did the only thing I could do to guarantee my distance from your mother—and you."

I waited, imagining the possibilities.

"I locked myself away, Mia."

I lightly gasped at the revelation.

He continued, "My embracer had the adequate accommodations for what I needed. ... And after a few years, the urgency and desire to seek her out and unite our blood began to decrease."

I felt fresh tears begin. "Years," I echoed, the word sounding so hollow.

"Alone in a room, closed off from both worlds. With only books and my painting to distract me. A meal brought to me when I could no longer postpone it." His eyes shifted as he recalled that time spent alone.

My heart began to race, a sudden sense of claustrophobia washing over me. The feeling increased as he continued. "I had no idea in that moment of saving your mother what I was condemning myself to." He recalled the darkest moments. My whole body stiffened. "I spent the first few weeks just pacing, reliving our encounter over and over. ..."

My hands began to shake. I clung to the armrests of the chair. His eyes slowly closed. "After that, all I felt was the emptiness, the aching to be near her. Protect her … know her in every way."

It was as if I were reliving the exact moment when Jennifer told me my parents were gone. The instinct I'd felt in that moment filled me too. I had wanted to run to them, find them. Felt being near them would help me somehow. Tears streaked my face, and I feared closing my eyes would result in seeing everything Sorin was seeing. I bit my lip, trying to pull myself from the sensation of spiraling into a deep dark abyss.

His eyes lifted open, and concern immediately covered his face. "Mia … are you ill?" He rushed to me, lifting me to my feet.

I tried to stand, catching my breath. "I can't hear about this anymore." The words came out in a rush as his arm slipped around my waist.

He helped me the few steps to the sliding patio door and closed it behind us. As effortlessly as he had before, he scooped me up and slowly carried me upstairs to my bed. I had stopped shaking and my breathing had returned to normal by the time Sorin placed me on the bed.

"I apologize, Mia … I did not realize my words … forgive me." He moved a pillow behind my head. The back of his hand caressed my cheek.

I sighed, beginning to feel myself again, just lethargic. "I'm okay … just drained." I looked up at him as he lit the candles around the bedroom. It took him less than a minute. "I felt everything you did all those years ago, Sorin … all the torment. I could never have imagined such a self-inflicted hell."

He paused, lighting the last candle, and kept his back to me. His shoulders slowly rose and fell. "I do not regret the decision to seclude myself … I only regret speaking of it to you. I was not mindful of your body already reacting to my actions."

It had not occurred to me until that instant. "Does that mean what I think it does?" A slight panic came over me. "Has a bond been made?" I asked, sitting up. "If I am feeling your emotions … have I become like you already?"

Sorin turned slowly, and before he spoke, his still deep-blue eyes showed disappointment in my concern. "No, Mia. … You may be feeling what I am emotionally and physically, but it is due to your blood currently in my system. You have not turned." He stepped to my side and sat on the edge of the bed. "I do feel that we are near the point of no return. … We should proceed with caution." He rested his hand over mine and lightly squeezed it. "That is, if you still have reservations about a future with me."

I wanted to say yes. Everything I was doing only increased a connection between us. I was sure choosing a future with him would happen eventually. But I couldn't take the final step off the cliff by saying it out loud. Instead, I chose to cruelly dance around it. It was so unfair to Sorin; how did he not hate me?

Is it inconceivable to hate someone who holds a part of you? I wondered.

Chapter 7

"Would you go back to that night and change it?" I asked, having wanted to ask him so times before.

"It cannot be done, and so I have never given it a thought. I made a choice that sealed my fate. For twenty-four years, that night has plagued me, driven me. It is the reason I am here with you. I do not want to live in the past. I am ready for a future, one with you in it." Sorin walked to his side of the bed and climbed in under the covers.

Just as I had many nights before, I felt overwhelmed and overstimulated. I took off my jeans but left my shirt on, and I slid under the covers next to him. I had wanted to be greeted with fiery violet eyes, to see all the worry had left him. I lay on my side, facing him.

Sorin scowled, brushing a few fingers along my chin. Much to my dismay, his eyes were a vivid blue. "Mia … what are your intentions?" he asked softly.

I shrugged at first, not completely sure. "I just want to be next to you. … Can't you see my intentions, feel them?" I offered back. Slipping my hand under his shirt, I rested it on his chest.

"The more our blood mixes, the more our feelings and emotions are the same. It is becoming more difficult to understand what I see around you." His fingers left my face.

"I just thought I would keep you warm tonight. Do you oppose?" I moved closer, molding my body to his. I rested my head into the crook of his arm and closed my eyes.

The arm I rested against encircled me, and he kissed my temple. "It is more complex than that, Mia, *amore*." His voice was so tender, and he inhaled deeply before resting his head back.

His words echoed in my mind. Sorin was right: my actions had become instinct. I wanted to be near him, craved his touch. Desired to feel his skin against mine. Visions of our flowery garden filled my thoughts, and my body reacted. My fingers began to explore his chest, making their way to his collarbone and tracing it delicately. "Take your shirt off," I said. "I want to feel your skin against mine." It was a hopeful request.

His arm tightened around me, and a strained moan escaped him. "Nothing more than that, Mia ... promise." He whispered against my forehead.

I pressed my hand against his chest as I sat up next to him. Finally, silver-blue eyes looked back at me as the candlelight danced off them. I began gently moving his shirt higher. "I just want to feel you next to me. Your skin against mine. I promise, nothing more." I spoke softly, helping him out the shirt.

He let it fall to the floor once free from it. Sorin's eyes quickly circled the air around me. Convinced of my innocent intentions, he lay back down.

The sight of him made my stomach flutter, but I intended on keeping my word. I would be content to simply lie next to him for the night. To lessen my temptation, I turned away from him and lay facing away after removing my shirt. Clearing my thoughts, I tucked my head back into the crook of his arm. He smoothly turned to his side and gathered me to him, his bare chest cool against my back. Sorin's hands stayed on my hip after positioning me perfectly against him. I sighed as his upper arm flexed under my face and he kissed my right shoulder.

"Is this acceptable?" Sorin's voice was just above a whisper, making a chill climbed my spine.

I softly shuddered next to him. "Beyond words," I said, closing my eyes. I reflected back on our conversation outside. "Is that why you go outside every night and pace indoors sometimes?" I recalled his restlessness at times.

"Mia?" he asked, confused.

"Do you pace sometimes due to locking yourself up in a room for so long? ... Do you feel claustrophobic often?" I inquired, suddenly sleepy.

"I do feel restless often ... enjoy not having walls around me when possible. It has been a short time since I closed myself off from the world. Those years in seclusion do affect me still. It was the correct path for me. ... But no more talk of those dark years."

His hand gently squeezed my hip, and I slipped my right hand to rest on his. I intertwined my fingers with Sorin's and guided his hand over my body. I paused at my stomach, wondering if he could feel the butterflies inside me. "I have not lain like this in so many years." He inhaled deeply at the top of my head and moaned softly. "You know my history ... should I worry about yours? How many Anyas are out there?" I bit my lip and waited.

He lightly laughed. "No need to worry ... or be jealous, love. I have only shared my blood twice. The first time was when I chose a new life; the second time was to save you. There have been women in my life over the years but only for temporary companionship. The last was long ago.

All brief and empty compared to what I feel now with you. None held a part of me as you do."

After a moment, I raised his hand higher, stopping just above my left breast. My heart pounded below his palm. "You cause that, Sorin," I confessed happily.

He kissed my shoulder again, but this time he made a short trail to my neck. My heart increased its rate, and my breath quickened.

"Should I cease? ... I realize how hypocritical I am being." His voice, low and silky, made me shudder. He kissed my neck again with lips parted slightly, tasting my skin this time. I quietly whimpered, pressing his palm harder into my chest. I could tell what he wanted, what his body still craved. Knowing I could give it, satisfy his thirst. I couldn't deny him.

Melting against him, I lowered my hand from where it rested just below my neck, placing it on Sorin's thigh. He kissed the same place on my neck, inhaling deeply. I tilted my neck, exposing the skin that surely filled his thoughts currently. The sound of him sucking in a quick breath confirmed it. I thought of how Sorin had looked as he bit my wrist earlier. The look of vulnerability, then pure hunger, then loss of control. My fingers dug into his upper leg, and I grabbed a handful of his pajama bottoms, twisting them in anticipation. I wanted to see his lips on my neck, to watch him fill himself on my blood. ...

I quickly moved away from him, kicking all the covers to the foot of the bed as I sat up.

Sorin quickly rose, sitting next to me. "I am sorry, Mia ... I should not have tried persuading you to ... I will stop." His words rushed out all at once.

I turned to him, twisting my body to face him. "Look at me. ... Do I want you to stop?" I barely heard my own words over the pounding in my ears.

Before his eyes could view the air around me, I threw myself at him, covering his mouth with mine. His arms quickly captured my upper arms, forcing some space between our bodies. He returned my kisses with obvious restraint. Before he had a change of heart, I pressed my tongue against an unsheathed fang. The metallic taste followed, but once it faded, I bit his lip, tasting him. Sorin's fingers pressed deeper into my bare arms, and I gasped at the unexpected pain. He pushed me away, and I was rewarded with the sight of desire-filled violet eyes burning into me.

I sat up and moved to the foot of the bed, with my back to him. My reflection centered perfectly in the mirror above the dresser across from me. I brought my knees to my body and crossed my ankles. I straightened my back and moved all my hair to the right side of my neck. It spilled over my shoulder, covering most of my breast. I looked at Sorin in the mirror and ran my hands over the bed around me in a circle. He moved forward until his legs framed mine, his bare chest lightly touching my back again. I let my knees fall away from one another, resting against his. I tilted my head to the side. He looked ahead at his reflection over my left shoulder.

"Continue," I whispered.

He hesitated, looking down at my neck momentarily. I watched Sorin's face in the mirror. Without looking away, I moved my hands from my lap, searching for his. I rested my right on his leg, just above his knee. He gently covered it with his right hand. Our left hands quickly joined as I spread my fingers and slipped them between his. Our eyes locked in the mirror as his body tensed around me.

"You realize, Mia … what could come of this?" His voice held a beautiful plea.

Forget stepping over the edge of an imaginary cliff. I was running blind and about to throw myself off. I knew exactly what I was doing, offering my blood yet again, tasting his earlier. I told myself nothing would change. I would be the same person hours from now. I watched his reflection, a thousand responses swimming in my head. I chose not to speak.

I brought our left hands up to my uncovered breast, pressing his palm to the heartbeat underneath. I leaned back and tried to relax against him. Sorin's eyes fell to my neck as he leaned forward, kissing me softly. My body molded to his, draining of any anxiety. I could feel every muscle in his body go rigid; he trembled slightly, trying to control himself. He nuzzled deeper into the curve of my neck. Sorin's kisses grew longer each time. He repeatedly inhaled my scent, lightly shuddering each time.

I closed my eyes and cleared my thoughts, concentrating on what Sorin was feeling. A wave of frustration came over me. Focusing on it, I felt more. A mixture of pure desire and anguish overcame me, and I gasped for air. My head spun, and all I could hear was my heart pounding. Sorin was torturing himself. Teasing his senses and refraining from indulging. My eyes flew open, besieged after feeling what he was experiencing.

I let go of his hand cupping my breast and reached up behind me, interweaving my fingers with a handful of Sorin's hair above the back of his neck. His eyes darted back to the mirror facing us, grabbing my right wrist as my fingers dug deeper into his leg.

The sight before me was breathtaking. Candlelight danced around us, catching his hungry eyes every few moments. I could smell roses from the nightstand. Our bodies looked perfect together, his mouth a breath away from my neck. I tightened my fingers around his hair and attempted to lower him to my neck. Sorin didn't move, but I felt his body react to my invitation.

"I'm sure," I said, hoping my words would make him let go.

His eyes fell to my neck once more. "Forgive me, Mia," his voice purred. "Forgive me for all I have done … you deserved so much more." His words fell on my skin, making it flush. A purely masculine moan reverberated through his chest just before his mouth descended. His fangs swiftly pierced my flesh, followed by his lips sealing around the sweet crimson extraction.

As before, I mostly felt pressure and very little pain. I tried to watch him drink me in. But after a few minutes, Sorin's eyes closed, and I began feeling sedated. His body relaxed, and his grip loosened on my wrist. Another few minutes, and I felt us both fading away. My eyes grew heavy, and he no longer filled my vision. Beautiful darkness claimed me.

Chapter 8

The sound of wind chimes woke me hours later. I blinked and stared at the ceiling above me. The wind caught the chimes again, and they sang loudly. I cursed, rolling toward Sorin lying next to me.

"Now the neighbors hung up wind chimes … they should have stayed lost in one of their boxes, never to be heard again," I complained, burying my face into his chest. He had tucked me under the covers with him and had retrieved his shirt while I slept.

Sorin's body lightly shook as he laughed. He moved my arm covering my head to dull the sound of the chimes. "Mia … that house has always had wind chimes."

I propped myself up on an elbow to glare at him. "We sit out there every night, and I have never seen or heard them," I said arrogantly, completely sure of myself.

Sorin's light smile faded. "The house I am referring to … is five doors down. That is the only house in the area with wind chimes." He brushed the back of his hand down my arm affectionately. "They are the chimes you hear right now." His eyes looked around me anxiously as he waited for my reaction.

It was naive of me to think I could dance on this line of indecision without its catching up with me. I lay back down, resting my head on his chest.

Sorin wrapped an arm around me, holding me tight. "Are you unhappy about this new … development?" He asked with light concern.

I closed my eyes and shrugged, not sure. I still felt like me. My heart was still beating in my chest. I hadn't turned yet. A little heightened sense of hearing shouldn't upset me. "I'm all right," I whispered.

Sorin was silent, and I eventually decided to get up. Sliding out from under the covers, I walked to my dresser. It was midday, to my surprise. Last night's events had thrown off my sleep pattern. Knowing Sorin couldn't go far, and with my wrist finally healed, I decided to run some errands. "I am going to meet with James from the pizzeria to show him what I have so far. Then maybe stop by the coffee shop and visit with the mama bears." I stopped gathering my clothes and looked up at the mirror.

He flashed a false smile. "Enjoy your day, Mia." His voice sounded hollow. I considered pressing, inquiring about his bleak mood. But I decided against it.

I went into the bathroom to take a shower. My sense of hearing wasn't limited to the wind chimes down the road. The water in the shower sounded like a roaring waterfall. I heard Sorin's phone ring and then his footsteps as he left the bedroom. I got out of the shower, dried off, and went back into my bedroom. It smelled of fresh smoke from his blowing out all the candles in the room. I dressed, noticing the bruises on my wrist and neck and smiling lightly.

I glanced into the front room as I reached the bottom of the steps: it was empty. I passed boxes of my parents' belongings sitting at the front door for donating. It was mostly clothes. I decided to call the number on the card that the nurse had given me for the women's shelter. I continued to the kitchen.

Sorin sat on his stool at the marble countertop. A plate of food and a steaming cup of tea were on the counter across from him. He didn't turn around or say anything as I entered the room. At moments like this, I wished he had colors around him to announce his mood. I circled around and sat across from him. Still silent, I began eating. It was clear his mind was elsewhere.

"Who called?" I asked, curious.

He looked at me, leaving his thoughts behind. "I will be away for a day or two. I need to visit an auction house and tend to some business." He seemed reluctant to inform me, or maybe he didn't really want to leave.

I felt anxious at the thought of his being anywhere but near me. My mood turned sour; he wasn't offering to take me with him. He didn't say where he was going, and I was not sure how long he was actually going to be away, as I hadn't heard him making plans for the trip while he was on the phone. Annoyed, I spoke up. "So your phone can sound like a siren is going off … but the conversation that follows is silent?" It didn't make sense to me that I hadn't heard a word.

Sorin straightened his back, frowning as he reminded me of the way things worked. "The emotional and physical bond to the one whose blood you are consuming forms first … your body will change last. It will come and go … for now at least. My blood is new to your body, so there will be a period of … adjustment. The transition is different for each human."

I finally understood his mood. I wasn't embracing the changes my body was experiencing; I was still refusing to commit to a life with him. But I had asked for his blood, increasing his vulnerability to me. I offered him myself over and over. I was sure it frustrated Sorin, understandably so.

I stood, sipping the last of my tea. Turning to the sink with my dirty plate in hand, I heard my teacup slide across the marble countertop. Before I knew it, I had spun around and caught it in midair; it rested perfectly in my palm. My eyes shot from the cup to Sorin, my own deft movement shocking me.

"Your hearing is not the only side effect from our ... crimson kisses, as you so eloquently put it," he told me. Laying a palm over his chest briefly, he let it drop. "Your heart rate has decreased also." Standing, he turned away. "I should only be a day or two, Mia."

He glanced back as I placed the teacup back on the counter. We both were unsure of what to say.

"Be safe," I finally whispered.

Sorin stopped at the dining room doorway. "The painting of our future is right in front of you, Mia. ... You only need to step back to see it clearly. Maybe while I'm away a decision will be easier to make." His voice drifted back to me, hanging in the air between us momentarily before he exited the room.

I wondered if the real reason for his trip was to pressure me into embracing a new life with him. I looked down at the two bruises on my wrist, delicately tracing them with my finger. They had become pale shadows already.

After cleaning up the kitchen, I went to the attic to paint. I kept raising the volume of my music higher and higher, wanting it to drown out my thoughts, but my new bionic hearing just made it deafening. After a few hours, I returned to the kitchen, retrieved James's phone number, and called to inform him I was close to finishing. I offered to come by to show him what I had done, and we set up a meeting for an hour later.

Then I found the business card for the women's shelter, called the number, and arranged to set out a few boxes of my mother's to be picked up. Returning to the attic, I heard the shower in the guest bath running as I passed the guest room. I continued on my way up to the attic, where I took multiple pictures of each painting with my digital camera. After paging through them, I was pleased. I left the attic, went back to my bedroom, and set the camera on my dresser.

My room was empty as I showered and dressed. I covered the bruises on my wrist with a fabric bandage that the nurse had given me. The bruises on my neck were a little more difficult to cover. I put on a light scarf, which looked silly, so I opted for on a chunky necklace instead. Leaving my hair down, I hoped no one would notice anything—especially the mama bears.

The guest room door was open as I passed it on the way to the kitchen. No Sorin; the same as I crossed the entrance to the front room. In the kitchen a bright square of paper on the refrigerator caught my attention right away. I quickly moved to it, but all it held was a phone number. I carefully peeked out a front window to the driveway. His SUV was gone. My heart sank. Looking up at the cloudy sky that threatened rain, I cursed. Between the darkening sky and his altered windows, he could safely leave. Trying to not continue thinking about it, I set out to meet with James.

A light mist began to fall just as I pulled into the pizzeria's parking lot. Once inside, I walked around, looking at how much had changed since I was last there. Just a few final touches, and it would be ready for customers. Workers moved around; a hostess folded bright-red napkins and put out silverware. A bartender slid wineglasses into place above the bar, and I cringed at the sound.

Eventually James found me and apologized for my wait. I showed him the pictures on my camera, and he was happy with them. After agreeing to be finished in two days, I left.

By then, the rain was pouring down. It was only the second time it had stormed like this since my parents' passing. I considered visiting them the next day; I had continued to put it off. My eyes watered as I tried to focus on the road through the downpour and rapid windshield wipers. Passing the coffee shop, I saw Jenny and Gina trying to lower the umbrellas over the outside tables. I pulled in and parked, drying my tears. I walked to the side door, letting the rain fall on me. I had always loved playing in the rain as a child. Even now, there was only a slight chill in the air. I hoped the rain would hide my recent tears.

I knocked hard on the metal door, and to my surprise, Kayla opened it.

A light smile showed on her face as she saw me. "You are soaked, Mia ... how long have you been knocking?"

I stepped inside onto the rubber mat. "A few minutes," I lied. "I must not have knocked hard enough." I shrugged as rain dripped from my hair and face.

Kayla grabbed a towel for me to dry off with.

"Thanks," I said, taking it from her. "I should have just gone in the front door. But there were customers." I suddenly felt silly standing there drenched.

Kayla looked to the front counter as clattering drifted back to us.

I overheard the sisters laughing. "Evelynn wouldn't have forgotten to lower the umbrellas and save the sugar from the rain." Gina tossed the wet sugar packets in the trash. "No, she was always the first to rush into a storm," she said, reminiscing.

I patted my hair and dried my face as Kayla began to look uncomfortable. "So … how are you doing?" she asked quietly.

I stilled my movements, multiple answers filling my head: *Better*; *Okay, I guess*; or *The pain has finally stopped, physically.* I closed my eyes and took a deep breath. "One day at a time," I eventually answered, forcing a smile. I began blinking back fresh tears.

Kayla weakly smiled in return. "I just read a quote that said, 'When the world caves in around you, only you can choose to dig yourself out.'"

I went back to drying myself while Kayla announced my arrival to her mother and Gina. "I heard Natalie tell my mother you were hurt." Kayla looked at my wrapped wrist, sling-free. "She was really worried about you." She spoke low enough to me that she wasn't overheard.

I offered my wrist and rolled it a few times. "Almost as good as new," I chirped. "It looked worse than what it really was." I gave a wink, trying to sell myself.

Thankfully, she relaxed and walked to the front counter. All three women were rain soaked and disposing of ruined sugar and creamer packets. Each briefly smiled, laughing about the chaos before me. I offered to help, but they refused. I shared how soon I was from being finished with my current paintings. They all congratulated me, saying how proud they were. I left feeling guilty about not coming sooner.

The rain had stopped, and the sky was even darker when I left. I wondered where Sorin was and what he was doing at that moment. I wanted to call him and tell him to return immediately. Then I felt frustrated over the urge to do so. Images of him filled my head, only making me feel more alone. No matter how hard I tried to not think about him, all my thoughts went back to Sorin. I placed a hand over my heart throughout the day when it ached randomly, wondering if it was Sorin that I felt.

I had no choice when it came to choosing a future with him: all that remained was just accepting my new life.

* * * * *

Once back home, I went straight to the attic and continued painting. I worked until my eyes burned, finishing the last painting for James. After a quick meal, I realized it was almost morning and set the boxes outside to be picked up. I happily crawled into bed, exhausted and with just enough energy to pull the sheet over myself.

The sun was just setting when I woke up. Making myself something to eat and taking it out onto the patio, I watched the sunset differently, knowing it was to be one of my last. My thoughts were of Sorin as the sky darkened, all our little moments together. The first time I heard his voice, his tricking me into eating, and how playful he had been with Scarlett. I wanted him to be upstairs waiting for me. Multiple times I had reached out for him as I slept, used to his being next to me and forgetting that for the first time in over a week he was gone. The sun finished falling behind the trees.

A door slammed shut, and Scarlett ran to her backyard. She began chasing fireflies and then noticed me. In less than a minute, she was at my side. "Hello," she said, beaming. Her bangs were so long, they almost covered her eyes.

"Hello." I smiled back.

Looking around, Scarlett's smile faded. "Where is he?" She was looking for Sorin.

"He's gone right now," I said, feeling heartbroken myself.

Turning to the backyard, she asked, "Do you know magic like he does?" Hope danced in her eyes.

"Magic?" I asked.

"Yeah … he said it was a secret. But he's your friend … so can you do the magic trick with the fireflies?" Once again her eyes sparkled at the possibility.

"No, Scarlett, I can't do the magic trick like Sorin. Sorry," I said, wondering when my movements would mimic his.

She looked at me, disappointed, and then, giggling, she quickly turned and continued pursuing the flickering lights in the air.

I admired the stars briefly before returning inside. After doing some extra cleaning of the kitchen and some laundry, I passed the front door and opened it to make sure the donations had been picked up. The boxes were now absent. It saddened me a little to know that soon almost all my parents' belongings would be gone. As I touched each item of theirs, I wondered when they had touched it last. My instinct was to keep almost everything. With each book, each article of clothing, a part of me cried to keep it. But nothing would be gained from that. They were just items once possessed by my parents. It wasn't them, and their things would not be able to bring my mother and father back to me. I forced myself to part with nearly everything. I shut the door and continued upstairs.

At the top of the stairs, I opened the door to my parents' room, leaning against the doorframe. There were boxes scattered throughout the room. Some still contained clothes of my father's to donate. A box sat to the side, gifts that the mama bears had given my mother over the years. The bed was still made and uncluttered. I sighed, eventually entering the room and walking around, looking at the boxes. My father's pile of sweaters called out to me. I sat on the floor and pulled out a few to keep, after all. Burying my face in them and inhaling deeply. It was bittersweet as I realized I would soon have use for his sweaters. My eyes watered, and I cried as I emptied the last of his closet. I moved the boxes downstairs and then opened the phonebook to find a donation center. I would call in the morning.

I went back up to the attic, wrapping all the finished paintings and setting them next to one another. I sat on the floor and admired the canvases Sorin had filled. I only owned a single empty canvas now. Picking it up, I envisioned the gazebo with flowers surrounding it. A few hours later, I was adding purple flowers to the canvas, remembering one of my mother's sundresses of the same color. Years before, she had worn it on vacation while we collected seashells on the beach. Once home, we'd made them into Christmas ornaments, covering the shells in paint and glitter. I finished painting the moonlit sky over the shadowed gazebo, feeling sleepy.

After cleaning my paintbrushes, I went back down to the kitchen. Sitting in the silence, I forced myself to eat. The curtain's edge fought sunlight. The cast-iron clock confirmed I had stayed up all night. I took a long bath and slipped into a satin nightgown. Climbing into bed and snuggling under the covers, I was saddened Sorin had stayed away another night. I admired the painting across from me, which now hung on the wall. Staring at the painting he had done in secret only worsened my mood. I rolled away from the image of myself. The bed smelled of Sorin, that wonderful sandalwood scent. Letting out a cry of frustration, I threw back the covers and climbed out of bed, restless and lonely.

Disgusted with my surroundings, I decided to sleep on the couch in the living room. I passed my parents' room and looked in. I had forgotten to shut their bedroom door earlier. The perfectly made bed invited me. I ran my fingers over the light quilt that covered it. Crawling into their bed, tears instantly filled my eyes. I hugged a rose-scented pillow and cried myself to sleep, wishing to be anywhere but here.

Chapter 9

Sleep claimed me, and soon I was deep in a dream. The sky was the bluest I had ever seen above me. Clouds filled it, light and airy. Lying in lush grass, I looked at the white puffs strangely not moving at all. Searching the sky more, I realized the sun was missing. Confused, I sat up and took in my surroundings. I sighed: Sorin's and my flowery garden. My heart ached at the beauty around me, and I pressed my palm into my chest. As if counterpressure over my heart would make the hurt ease. I slowly stood and saw I was wearing my nightgown.

I slowly closed my eyes each time I changed multiple details. A light breeze began. My nightgown melted away into a deep-crimson strapless gown flowing behind me. The cool wind made my hair dance around my shoulders as I walked around the garden. The butterflies were absent, and I decided against picturing them. My mood was somber, turning the colors of the flowers around me. The purples darkened to almost black, and the blues turned a wine color. The sky darkened, and a full moon filled it. No birds chirped, no crickets sang; just silence. The garden that had been so bright and colorful now looked dark and tortured. But it was still beautiful as I walked around, touching the flowers. I was in awe of what I had created, the colors and the projection of my mood.

Never wanting to leave this dream, I wished for Sorin to be there with me. My heart leaped and joy filled me. To feel sadness and someone else's joy at the same time was overwhelming. I pressed my hand against my chest. Wherever he was, Sorin was happy.

I wanted to cry as I left the deep-red roses and almost-black irises near the gazebo. I walked to the weeping willows moving in the breeze. Morning glories twisted around their trunks. I leaned close to touch one the color of the fabric I wore. Just as the tip of my finger touched it, the flower closed. It caught me by surprise, and I jumped at the movement. I reached out to another near it. It quickly closed just before I touched it. I stood up, completely baffled at the flower's actions.

Sorin chuckled behind me, and my heart raced at the sound. I spun around, and there he stood, only a few feet behind me. He wore his thin ebony pajama bottoms and the breeze around us warmed. Sorin's arms were crossed over his chest, and a mischievous grin played on his lips. I stood for a minute, not knowing what to do. Was he real, or had I just wanted him with me so much that he appeared in my dream? I considered trying to wake up, on the chance that he had finally returned. But I thought of the heartache that I would feel if I discovered he was still away.

Just then, Sorin held out a hand for me to join him. I hurried toward him, closing the space between us and wrapping my arms around him. He felt so good, I was afraid to let go. I nuzzled my face in his neck, sighing as I smelled sandalwood.

Sorin lightly laughed. "Do you come here often without me?" he whispered near my ear. He spoke with such affection, it touched me.

Worried he would evaporate before me, I kept my arms around him, only moving my face enough to look at him. "Are you really here?" I swallowed nervously. "Or am I just imagining you … like everything else?"

His light smile faded, and I felt anxious. Sorin reached up and cupped the side of my face. He looked into my eyes in the way that made my very soul feel exposed. Sorin guided my face to his as he quietly said, "You tell me, Mia … am I real?" His lips pressed into mine as I sighed in pleasure. He continued kissing me softly, coaxing my lips apart to taste me further. My fingers left his neck and entangled in his hair, keeping him close. A whimper left me as his kisses lowered to my chin, then the curve of my jaw. "I missed you greatly." His voice lightened my head, all thoughts diminishing. "I missed the smell of you." He inhaled just below my ear. A chill climbed my spine, and I shivered against him. "I craved the taste of you." His voice was so velvety, I began to fade away. Sorin's breath moved to the sweep of my neck. "I craved the sensation of you stirring in my blood, moving within me." I felt his deep kiss begin. My knees instantly went weak, and I collapsed against him. Sorin's arm wrapped around my waist, supporting me. His mouth departed from my neck, and he delicately kissed the skin he had just pierced. "Tell me you missed me, Mia." Another kiss, just above the fresh wound. "Did you yearn for me … as I did for you?" His pale-blue eyes searched my face. I had no doubt that I was desperate for him to be here with me.

I found my footing and took a step back. "Can't you see what I am feeling?" My heart beat faster as my fear increased, wondering if his presence was real.

"There are no colors around you here, Mia." Tears began to fill my eyes; he had failed to mention that the last time we were here together. Concern crept over his expression. "I feel it," he said adoringly, closing his eyes as he stood before me. "I feel how content you are since my return, the way your heart aches now." He opened his eyes, stepping closer. "I do not question how you feel … I simply desire to hear you say the words." Sorin's hand caressed my face, his thumb brushing across my lips.

I couldn't hold the tears back any longer. As I buried my face in his chest, tears poured out of me. "I did, Sorin… so much that it overwhelmed me at times. I'm afraid that I am imagining all this just to ease some of the loneliness I felt. I should wake up and end my torture!" I exclaimed.

His arms tightened around me. "No, Mia, stay here with me," he pleaded. "Let's not leave just yet." Sorin gently untangled my arms from around his waist. He guided me to the lush grass below and sat at my side. Looking around the garden, his shoulders fell a little. "It is darker than I remember," he said, pointing out the obvious, acknowledging the differences.

I looked around at all the dark-colored flowers and the moon less bright than last time. "It matched my mood." I shrugged.

He lifted my hand, kissing it. "I will prove you are not imagining my presence."

I wiped my cheeks dry.

He looked deep in thought for a moment, and then he lovingly smiled. "I will describe the first time I saw you." His eyebrows rose, hopeful. I frowned. "A crumpled Mia on the dining room floor."

I sniffed. "I don't think I wish to relive that moment, even through your eyes, Sorin." My words made his increase.

He brushed away the last of my tears. "I had seen you earlier that day." Feeling confused, I straightened my back, interested. His eyes glazed over as he recalled that moment, the smile abandoning him. "You stood over your parents' graves. Tears assaulting your porcelain skin …

anguish in your eyes. Jennifer held your hand, and her husband covered the two of you with an umbrella all the way to the car." I fought new tears, remembering those first steps away from my mother and father. "I saw something no one else did, Mia." He focused on me again and reached out for my hand closest to him. "As you walked to the car, you held your hand out from under the umbrella. You wanted to feel the rain on your skin." Sorin placed my hand over his and then traced it with his other hand. "You wanted that rain to wash away the pain that filled you." He looked into my eyes again. "You would have stood there in the rain happily for the prospect of some relief, yes?"

All I could do was nod a yes. He was here, really here, and I felt it. He leaned in and kissed me as I closed my eyes, cherishing the reunion with Sorin. I gasped as rain fell on me unexpectedly. My eyes opened; the sky had darkened, and lightning flashed silently over us. Thunder never sounded, but the ground beneath us lightly shook. I raised my face, enjoying the feeling of droplets on my skin. The air around us was still warm. Sorin stood and helped me up. The thin fabric of my dress began to cling to me, darkening as the rain soaked it. Pulling me to him, he tasted my rain-covered lips. I slowly traced the lines on his chest with my fingers. His body tensed under my touch. The sky darkened further, and lightning crackled loudly. I jumped, my heart racing.

Sorin's arms encircled my hips, pressing me close. His kisses became aggressive, and a low growl rumbled in his chest. "I love the sound and feel of your heart racing." His mouth traced my neck to my shoulder in a heated trail. Returning to my lips, he paused briefly, tasting me again. "Please, Mia." His voice was low and hoarse. "Free me from this torture. … Say yes."

My eyes flickered open, and lightning lit the black sky above. Sorin's eyes searched mine for an answer. Turning away, I squeezed my eyes shut, wanting to stay in the moment. I wanted this sense of euphoria to continue as long as possible.

"You have decided. ... Why deny it?" I could hear the strain in his voice.

I knew in that moment Sorin was minutes away from sealing our fate. He only wanted me to give permission, as a way of easing his conscience. My heart pounded in my ears for the last time, and his voice barely registered.

"You have possessed a part of me for years now, Mia. ... Will you not claim the rest?" I bit my lip, wanting to scream yes. *"Si prega di amore mio ... fine nostra sofferenza."*

Even though I only understood a few words, the Italian was beautiful, and I finally agreed. "Yes," I said, just above a whisper.

He froze, his lips almost touching mine. "Yes?" he asked, a tormented ache in his voice.

I nodded, feverishly kissing him.

Sorin scooped me up, carrying me to the gazebo and laying me down before him. He pulled away, ending our embrace. I softly cried a protest and reached out for him to return. He faced me, sitting at my side. His fingers traced my collarbone, and we both sucked in a quick breath. I smiled, knowing it was for different reasons.

Sorin's eyes locked with mine. "I want to see you ... one more time before you no longer possess all human traits." His voice was a little sad. I frowned, not understanding his words. He kissed me lightly. "I want to see you bathed in colors of gold." His sultry voice made me blush as I understood. I nodded my consent. His hand began its descent down my body.

I abruptly grabbed it, stopping him. "You said you couldn't see colors here." I was suspicious and started to sit up. "You did say that," I pointed out before Sorin could even try to explain.

He lightly smiled and eased me onto my back again. "Relax … *fidati di me amore.*" His fingers followed the curves and lines of my body. The way his hand moved, it was obvious I had put some weight back on. Following the curves of my chest, his fingers dipped less over my stomach. I wondered what Sorin thought as I watched his eyes follow his touch. Now calm, I moved my head his direction. "Now close your eyes, Mia." His voice warmed my skin where his words fell. I obeyed, my eyelids heavy. He kissed my temple and whispered slowly, "Keep your eyes closed and concentrate on my touch." My head lightened further as he spoke. The sound of rain ended and the heavy scent of flowers passed. He gently squeezed my calf and then my thigh.

Sorin took his time moving his hand higher. I slowly writhed beneath him, grabbing at the sheets. My body tensed a short time later as the glorious waves intensified. I quietly repeated Sorin's name, pleading for my release. He lightly kissed me and remained near. "Say it again, Mia … tell me you want a life with me, love." His voice melted into me, his touch slowing as encouragement to answer. I bit my lip and twisted in frustration. "Convince me, Mia." His alluring voice pulled me closer. "Convince me, and I will have golden sunburst around you momentarily … I promise."

I whimpered and let every enclosed thought pour from my lips. "Yes!" I softly exclaimed. "I am done with this life, Sorin … help me embrace another. One with you." His exquisite affection quickened its pace. I felt the warmth from his mouth through the fabric of my dress just above my heart, cupping the breast he now lingered over. I continued, my voice strained. "I cannot imagine another day without you next to me or another night without you near."

My back arched as Sorin kept his promise. I heard his voice off somewhere in the distance as my body shook softly.

"You will know neither far as long as I live, Mia." As my name left his lips, the breast he so tenderly cupped was pierced by his fangs.

I gasped at the sensation and arched my back more, without any thought. I cried out when the pressure and pain doubled in a flash. I could no longer keep myself asleep in my fantasy garden. My eyes shot open, and I blinked a few times, overcome by pleasure and pain simultaneously. I was in my own bed; Sorin had moved me, I realized. Maybe when he carried me to the gazebo in our garden. The feeling of bliss faded, and I winced. His bite had never been this intense—or this deep. I tried to push him away. But no sooner did I attempt to do so than Sorin's hands moved to just above my elbows, holding me down. The more I resisted, the tighter his grip became. Adrenaline rushed through me, and a few tears of fear moistened my face.

Sorin forced himself from my chest, looking down at me. My blood ran cold, and I froze. His eyes were ablaze, the light from the hallway catching them in the dark room. They were a deep red, brilliant maroon. Before I could end what was to follow, his mouth covered my cry.

It began forceful, aggressive, his tongue plunging past my lips. The strong taste of my own blood alarmed me. I screamed at myself to trust him, to allow it all. Kissing him back worked, as he loosened his grip on my upper arms. Sorin's kisses softened. Any doubt of my safety or his intentions vanished. He finally pulled himself away and released my arms completely. His eye color had hardly changed as he looked toward the nightstand. In an effortless movement, he retrieved a single rose. Excitement and anxiety filled me, as I knew his intention. He held the rose in one hand and caressed my face with the other. Sorin delicately pinched my chin, guiding my lips apart.

I swallowed hard, trying to ease the lump in my throat. He repositioned his wrist over my mouth and lowered the rose to his flesh. "The wound will heal quickly, Mia … take as much blood as you can." I nodded, unable to speak a simple yes. He took the thorn and tore at his skin.

Sorin's blood seeped into my mouth. The tiny burst of crackling began as I had experienced before. I raised a hand, lowering his wrist and completely lifting my head from the bed. I thrust my tongue at the cut, hoping to delay the healing, sucking greedily. After a few gulps, the tickling bursts in my mouth changed. I cringed as it felt like needles were pricking my throat. I squeezed my eyes shut, trying to imagine Sorin's and my garden. Trying to take my mind elsewhere, I achieved a few flashes of flowers and nothing more. Another mouthful of his blood, and it was as if I had swallowed liquid fire. My whole body screamed in shock. I threw my head back into the pillow below me, letting go of his wrist as the pain only intensified. Spasms began throughout my body, and I twisted, facing the painting Sorin had done. I couldn't help but cry out in agony, pulling my knees higher. Rocking back and forth I clawed at the comforter underneath me. I reached for Sorin, wanting to be comforted if possible.

He had left my side. I opened my eyes, searching the room for him. The light from the hall was weak. He stood in the bathroom doorway, his back to me. Did he regret his actions already? I fought the pain as it reached my extremities. Sorin collapsed to the floor, sitting and facing me. He wrapped his arms around his midsection and began to sway. He stared at the floor between us. Another flood of pain made me wail, and I reached out to Sorin. He denied me with a slow shake of his head. I didn't understand how he could be so cruel, and I began to cry. The waves of agony kept on, and I buried my face into a pillow, muffling the horrible sounds escaping me. Every part of my body felt like hot needles flowed through it. I looked at Sorin, hunched over and gritting his teeth.

I called out for him, begging for him to come to me. I reached out again. He was a blur gathering me to him. I had thought the pain had reached its peak, but I was wrong. As Sorin's arms encircled me, I almost blacked out from the agony. He had only kept his distance to spare me some of the misery. He was feeling everything I was, and it only intensified the closer he was to me. Which was worse: to lie alone in pain, or to feel his arms around me and intensify that pain for both of us? Sorin rested my head against his chest and held me tight. I lay in Sorin's arms, crying, and my body lurched as spasms took over.

"*Shhh* ..." he finally whispered. "Try not to fight it, Mia ... it will eventually pass." He kissed the top of my head. "We will suffer together, love. ... I will stay with you until the pain subsides." His voice cracked lightly as his tear fell on my shoulder.

Realizing this pain was not mine alone gave me the strength to welcome it. Sorin gently swayed, rocking me in his arms, and I tried to suffer quietly. I took deep breaths and thought of our peaceful garden once more. I heard my heartbeat thud loudly. *Thump ... thump ... thump.* It should have been racing in my chest. But many seconds passed between each contraction. The waves of misery gradually slowed, and I tilted my head back to kiss Sorin. Sweetly kissing me back, he lowered me to the bed, showering me with kisses. The needles came farther and farther apart now. My whole body had a dull ache to it. I turned to my side and rested my head on his upper arm. He gathered me close, spooning me.

Content the worst was over, I closed my eyes. Sorin draped his free arm over my waist protectively and planted a kiss on my shoulder. We simply lay in silence, enjoying the closeness now felt. I knew the right decision had been made. The feeling of loneliness—the feeling something within me was missing—was now absent. I was aware of the inevitability of this outcome, and I rolled to face Sorin.

He kept his hand on my waist and kissed my cheek. "Recovered?" he asked.

I nodded and looked into his eyes, now their usual ice blue. "I have been waiting for you my whole life, Sorin. ... I just didn't know it until now. I never had a choice, did I?" I kissed him softly.

"No, Mia," he said, remorseful.

I sighed. "So now what?" I looked at him and smiled lightly. "No sun, no food, no eight hours of sleep for me?"

Sorin remained silent. "I am just glad that it's over." His expression changed. "You are not who you were hours ago, but it will take another exchange or two of blood for your body to completely change. I have told you that ... remember." He caressed my cheek.

I had forgotten, and my body tensed at the very thought of repeating what I had just experienced.

Sorin gave me a light squeeze. "Do not fret, love … it will not match the pain of the first time."

I relaxed, relieved at the news. I licked my lips, the taste of his blood still heavy in my mouth.

"Want to get some fresh air?" His tone was light, and he fought a grin.

It wasn't a simple question, obviously. Intrigued, I slid from the bed and brushed my teeth. Sorin stepped into the doorway as I finished, and I blushed, a little embarrassed. "Guess I have to get used to the taste."

Sorin looked at my reflection in the bathroom mirror. "Soon you will crave the taste, Mia," he stated, turning away.

A moment later, I heard him dressing in the other room as if he were right next to me. I chuckled and changed my own clothes.

Chapter 10

The steps creaked as I descended, which I'd never noticed before. I went into the kitchen, poured myself a glass of milk, and started to drink it. It tasted different than usual, so I dumped it down the sink. I actually heard it drain through the pipes below me. I lifted the tap handle to rinse out the glass, quickly slamming it back down because it sounded like a small waterfall.

Sorin laughed softly behind me.

I spun around in surprise. "So the faucet can sound like roaring water to me, but I can't hear you come up behind me!"

He smiled and shrugged. "I can be much quieter than water." He winked. "Especially if I'm trying to be quiet. All acquired abilities increase with age. And are at their peak after feeding." He walked through the kitchen, stopping at the doorway to the back hall. His smile faded, and he held a hand out for me to follow him. "Time to desensitize you, Mia." His voice expressed that he was serious.

I slipped my hand into his as we proceeded down the hallway. "That does not sound pleasant," I moaned.

Just before sliding the patio door open, he teased, "You can come back in when it overwhelms you."

Once I stepped outside, all was understood. Crickets announced their presence. A loud buzz from a mosquito made me swat at the air. Knowing it was probably many feet away, I stopped. I could hear the wind whistle through trees an acre away. Then a mouse squeaked, and I jumped. Frustrated, I cursed and covered my ears. Sorin stepped in front of me, placing his hands over mine. I frowned and let out a low whine.

With both our hands over my ears, the sound boomed in my head, and I jerked my hands away. "How do you do this?" I asked, exasperated.

He raised an eyebrow and leaned in near my ear. "It is not all bad, Mia." His voice was seductive. His fingers moved ever so lightly up my arms, over my shoulders, and then back down. I shuddered at his gentle touch, sighing as visions of Sorin filled my mind. He let out a low moan and moved away.

"What?" I complained, upset by his sudden distance.

He continued to the steps that led to the backyard. "Do not rush it, Mia ... it will be a while before that is even a possibility."

I crossed my arms, annoyed. "You offered," I grumbled, starting after him.

He turned and scowled at me. "I offered nothing ... I was simply changing your focus from sound to touch. It will be some time until your body fully adjusts. For now, you need to get used to your surroundings; you need to try to control everything that is flooding your senses. Focus on one sense at a time, or dance between two—three at the most—as I just showed you. Otherwise, it will be overpowering. Smaller amounts of stimulation will be much more tolerable. You will eventually be able to handle the heightened acuity of all five of your senses."

Listening to him, I realized it had actually worked. The noise faded, and the wind seemed to caress my skin. I stepped into the grass and felt every blade slip between my toes. Even the slight sinking of the ground below my feet registered. As I watched Sorin increase his distance, I wondered just how sensitive he was after having his blood so recently consumed. I stopped walking, mischievous intentions filling my thoughts. His pace slowed, and he glanced over his shoulder briefly.

Clearly, emotions were translating between us. I smirked, confident I would be successful.

I concentrated on Sorin's back in front of me. Reaching behind myself, I slipped my hand under my shirt as high as I could, raking my nails across my back. I watched as he halted midstep, his back arching forward. I laughed lightly as I easily heard him let out a sound of frustration. He slowly turned around, and the moonlight caught his eyes. The silver-blue pools only showed me I was unsuccessful in what I was trying to accomplish. I lifted the front of my shirt, exposing my stomach. Sorin's eyes narrowed on me, and a look of warning covered his face. Biting my lip, I was excited as I placed my left hand on the opposite side of my abdomen. No sooner had my fingers begun to slide across my skin than there was a blur in my direction. I yelped, as within seconds, Sorin had me flat on my back and pinned on the ground. I chuckled and saw him fighting a smile himself.

"No games, Mia," he ordered, gently balanced over me.

I silently pondered my possibilities. I lifted my head from the grass, trying to kiss him.

He easily avoided the contact. "You are still ... a teacup." He finally smiled. "In many ways you are still delicate, love. I will not risk breaking you again. Be patient ... not much longer." He delivered the lightest kiss to my lips and quickly stood.

I stayed on the ground, not sure I wanted to be defeated so easily.

Sorin looked down at me, offering his hand to help me up. "You will not win this fight, Mia. ... I refuse to bend in this area. You will only frustrate yourself in any further pursuits of intimate affection." He tried to sound firm.

A subtle bitter taste began, and I tapped my lips with my index finger. He understood the white lie was still tasted, and a few lines grew on his brow. I took his hand, wondering which part he hadn't completely believed himself. We walked to the tree line. The blades of grass continued to prick my feet. At one point, I stepped on a worm, letting out a disgusted sound as it squished beneath my foot. Once at the trees, he encouraged me to focus on all the different senses at once. It quickly became overwhelming, just as Sorin had predicted. The scent of everything that passed in the air. The feel of the tree bark under my fingers. I could hear the wind chimes from many houses away, as if I held them in my hands.

He could tell it was becoming too much, and we headed back to the house. He placed an arm around my waist, and I lay my head against his shoulder, feeling drained. Back inside, I walked to the refrigerator out of habit, as my stomach had rumbled a moment before. Sorin sat on his stool, watching me. Opening the fridge sent a rush of aromas in my direction. I covered my face with my hand to keep from gagging.

I slammed the door shut and turned around. "That is awful!" I complained. "It did not smell like that an hour ago." My voice was muffled through my hand.

Sorin frowned in compassion. "Try not to take in all the scents at once ... center your attention on one item. It should help." His voice was encouraging.

I reluctantly lowered my hand. Soon the wonderful scent of sandalwood overcame me. I opened my eyes and smiled. "That is much better," I said, sitting on a stool across from Sorin. I looked over my shoulder at the fridge. "Does this mean my … diet has changed?" The smell of food had made my stomach turn; I couldn't imagine eating anything.

Sorin shrugged lightly. "Everyone responds differently after being exposed to our blood. For some, it takes very little to fully turn. The transformation is unique for each human. Be cautious … I can sense many changes already. If you do eat, stay away from anything processed." He nodded toward the refrigerator. "If food is unappealing, it may be due to your digestive system changing already; your body may reject what it disapproves of." His expression turned somber, and I felt his mood change. "Mia, I know how you feel about the subject … but it has reached a point of necessity." I frowned, not knowing what he meant, but feeling his apprehension. "Soon your appetite will be for blood alone. If you wish for me to be the only one you taste … I will happily oblige." He paused, and I understood the point of the conversation. "But we cannot continue to feed on one another only. Without new nutrients from fresh blood we will make ourselves ill." Sorin explained it as delicately as he could.

I raised a hand, halting his words. It made sense we couldn't sustain each other. One of us would have to fill our hunger elsewhere. "How soon?" I asked flatly.

His shoulders fell slightly, and his voice lowered. "I could spend a few hours away tonight while you paint." His eyes looked in the direction of the attic. "You should really finish your paintings and turn them over to Mr.Szurpicki. Your tolerance for the sun will decline rapidly. You will need to start doing everything after sunset, Mia."

I didn't share that I had finished the paintings already. With my appetite thoroughly ruined, I excused myself. As I left the kitchen, I asked, "You will be back by morning, right?"

Sorin smiled softly as he followed me. "I promise, love."

I began preparing my supplies for a few hours of painting and heard the front door close. I told myself it was something I was going to have to get used to. Hearing his vehicle start and then leave, I picked up the painting of our garden that I had begun the night before. It looked very different to me now. I saw colors meeting each other exactly where they blended. Reaching out, I touched it, running my fingertips over it slowly. I was amazed at how every brushstroke felt to my touch. Finding every flaw, I decided to repaint the entire thing.

I recalled what Sorin had said about my soon not being able to go outdoors during the day. So many questions filled my head. How soon would I truly be like him? Could I feed from someone other than Sorin? I thought of all the new sensations I was experiencing and couldn't wait to discover more. I took my time with the painting. Hours passed, and I felt tired. I heard the shower turn on below me. I had been so focused on my painting that I had failed to hear him return.

Quickly putting everything away, I hurried downstairs to my room. Sorin was already stepping out of the guest room as I passed it. I threw my arms around him, and our lips met briefly. He tasted different this time, and he smelled of cheap aftershave. I stepped back.

"You taste different," I complained.

"It will fade eventually," Sorin assured me.

I wrinkled my nose. "You smell different too," I fussed.

"I just showered, Mia." His voice began to rise in frustration. "I happened upon a frat party at the university a few towns over. ... He won't remember anything in the morning." I quickly smiled and tried to back him toward my room.

"Maybe you just need another shower," I suggested seductively.

Sorin didn't budge. I would have been more successful relocating a stone wall. The scowl faded from his face. "Well, next time I will be sure to hold out for someone who smells more appealing ... a nice floral or fruity scent. The more innocent they are, the sweeter they taste," he quipped.

I pushed him and turned to go downstairs. When the initial irritation wore off, I realized he had said it purposely to change my mood. I continued down the steps, upset that the image of Sorin's mouth on some female college student was enough to slay any romantic notions.

We curled up on the couch together, and he flipped through the channels on the television. Content, I lay in his arms for hours in silence. My eyes started to drift shut when I felt groggy.

He gave me a gentle nudge and nodded to the stairs. "To bed with you," he whispered.

"Only if you join me."

He shut off the television and led me upstairs.

Sorin pulled the covers back for me, and I climbed into bed. I smiled to myself afterward; I was starting to feel chilled. Sorin lit a few candles and then joined me moments later. My eyes were heavy, and I fought to keep them open as he looked down at me, a light smile on his face. He brushed aside a few stray curls, and I drifted off.

I dreamed I was in the attic and a painting sat in front of me. It was of a young woman. Nude with sandy blonde hair, she looked at her reflection in the mirror, from the waist up. She was brushing her hair with a golden hairbrush that had intricate design on it. Her right hand reached over to brush the hair draped over her left breast. Behind her was a stone window frame that her hair trailed out of. I sat up, wide awake and inspired by a vision of Rapunzel's reflection.

I had talked to the mama bears at the coffee shop about starting that new set of paintings for them. And my dream gave me the perfect idea for what to paint. I looked over at Sorin. He was sitting against the wall next to me, a look of surprise or curiosity on his face. "I know what I'm painting for the coffee shop."

I kept a sketchbook and a few pencils on the corner of my dresser for moments like this. I scrambled out of bed to collect them. Picking them up, I stopped when I saw the time. I had only slept for a few hours, but I felt fully refreshed. Pleased, I crawled back into bed and began drawing. Sorin watched over my shoulder.

"Natalie had the idea for me to do a different nude figure for each astrological sign," I explained to Sorin. "But I just had a dream of a young woman looking in the mirror and brushing her blonde hair. In the background you could see her hair trailing out a stone window. It was Rapunzel," I continued, excited. "Instead of astrological signs, I am going to paint young women from fairy tales. Each nude, but with minimal skin showing." I drew some more and pointed at the image. "Like Rapunzel here. Her reflection is from the waist up. But her arm brushing her hair covers most of her exposed breast."

I flipped the page and rapidly sketched some more. A drawing of Briar Rose asleep on her bed appeared. Blonde curls covered the pillow she lay on. A blanket rested at her waist, and her arms crossed over her chest. Each palm rested over a bare breast. I quickly flipped the page again.

"I think a close-up of Snow White biting into an apple. A cute little bob haircut and her eyes closed. A deep royal-purple background, and the bright-red apple at her lips. Then her bare shoulders and collarbone will be a beautiful contrast to the dark, rich color behind her." I looked at Sorin, my mind racing with ideas. A few minutes later, I admired my third drawing.

He smiled and touched the newest drawing, following Snow White's jawline to the apple in her hands. "Make this one a self-portrait." He said it as a request, not a suggestion.

I shrugged. "Okay," I agreed and flipped the page, starting a drawing of a mermaid.

He sat and watched me as more ideas spilled from my pencil onto the paper. An hour later, I had drawn out a handful of sketches, all young women from fairy tales. It was still too early to call James to set up a time for him to collect his paintings, I excused myself and headed upstairs to the attic, eager to get all the images onto canvas. Once in the attic, I remembered that all my canvases had been used and I would need to go get more. I ripped the drawings from my book and spread them out around me.

Deciding on the colors for each painting, I moved tubes of paint to each drawing. Almost every painting was going to be done in light or pastel colors. The bedding for Briar Rose was going to be a pale pink.

Rapunzel's painting was almost all gray stone behind her, with her golden hair covering her. I wanted to paint gold or bronze in each painting somehow. Rapunzel's hairbrush, a necklace on Snow White, and a comb in Briar Rose's hair. I was out of both metallic colors. The store wasn't open yet, but I didn't mind waiting a short time. I would be the first customer of the day. I returned to my bedroom and started to dress.

Sorin leaned forward in the bed. "What are you doing, Mia?"

Grabbing clothes, I mumbled, "I need to go to the store to get some supplies. Canvases and metallic paints. I won't be long." I slipped into my jeans.

"You cannot be serious." His tone made me pause and look at him. "You don't know how you'll react to the sunlight. Your heart has slowed, you are sleeping less, and your reflexes have improved. You need to start going out after dark."

I looked away from him. "The store will be closed by dark," I pointed out. I finished dressing slowly and guided my feet into some nearby sandals. He was right; I had not considered the possibility of the sun affecting me already. "It could be fine," I said, hopeful.

Sorin lay back against the wall with a thud, unhappy about my choice. "Well, you will know right away, Mia." He rubbed his head, frustrated. "As will I," he said under his breath.

I winced; if the sun caused me pain, he would feel it. It was a new concept sometimes forgotten. I sat on the edge of the bed. This would definitely take some getting used to, always remembering that from now on my actions wouldn't only affect me. I thought of the paintings some more. Bubbling inside, giddy and excited about creating my own art again. I sat still, trying to convince myself all would be well if I stepped outside.

But I realized how guilty I would feel if I caused Sorin avoidable physical pain.

Sorin let out an annoyed grumble and motioned to the door. "Just go." He shook his head. "I suppose you will learn how the sun feels sooner or later … we all do." He crossed his arms. I flashed a forced smile and darted out the bedroom door.

Chapter 11

My stomach growled as I reached the kitchen counter and retrieved my car keys. I looked at the refrigerator but decided not to open it. I pulled some organic crackers from the cupboard and went to the front door. Suddenly nervous, I paused before opening it. Peeking outside from behind a curtain, I didn't feel anything. I stepped out slowly, still cautious, not sure what I was waiting to feel.

I drove to the store, and shortly after I arrived, an employee opened the doors. We exchanged good mornings, and it didn't take long for me to pick out what I needed. I purchased canvases that would fit in my car, so no delivery was necessary.

I drove slowly through town, passing the coffee shop as Jennifer and Natalie set up tables outside for the day. I pulled in to help them. "Good morning, mama bears." I called out.

Both turned and smiled, happy to see me. I walked up to Jennifer and hugged her. As I stepped back, she looked surprised at the gesture. Which in turn made me realize it was a little out of character for me to initiate a hug.

Thankfully, Natalie looked past me and could see the canvases in my car. "You're starting the set of paintings?" She seemed so pleased.

I smiled. "Yes … and as wonderful as your idea was, I went in a little different direction. But the next series will be the astrological signs, for sure." It was true, and Natalie smiled.

"So what did you choose as your subject for this set?" Jennifer asked.

I started helping them open the umbrellas over the tables. "I had this vivid dream about Rapunzel brushing her hair in front of a mirror."

Both women seemed to approve, and I began describing each painting as we set out packets of sugar and creamer for each table.

Natalie laughed. "Almost all of those involve a prince rescuing a damsel in distress. Don't we all want our prince to come along? I thought I had one ... but it turned out he was a frog."

I had forgotten she was recently divorced. I stopped. "I never thought of it like that." Maybe unknowingly Sorin had been my inspiration. I followed them inside, where the scent of walnuts greeted me. "What are you making with black walnuts?" I asked, curious. Both women looked at each other, then at me.

"I grabbed the wrong bag of walnuts for cinnamon rolls ... but that was two mornings ago, Mia." Natalie sounded surprised and smelled the air herself. An awkward silence filled the room, and Natalie excused herself to fill the baked-goods display case.

Jennifer's expression made me feel a little uncomfortable, and I decided to head home. "Well I'd better be going ... paintings to start." I smiled and started toward the door.

She followed me to the car. Before I could open my car door, Jennifer put her hand on it, stopping me. "Are you doing okay? ... I mean do you need to tell me something? You can confide in me, you know." She spoke softly, despite no one else being around us.

"I am ... adjusting." I smiled at the multiple meanings of the sentence. "Thank you for everything you have done these past weeks. Really ... words cannot express my gratitude to you and Gina. You all have done so much." I expected her to hug me or tear up ... something. But as I talked, she just watched me and slowly frowned, looking confused.

"How are you feeling ... really?" Jennifer stepped back and looked me over.

"Why?" I asked.

"You seem different today, that's all." She sighed and shrugged. "I can't decide what it is exactly, Mia. I am happy if you have finally found some peace. I just worry you are rushing it or forcing it maybe." She gave me a light hug and headed back into the building.

I climbed into the car and called James, informing him he was welcome to retrieve his paintings anytime. He said he would send an employee with a truck and moving blankets to wrap them with shortly.

I arrived home a few minutes later, taking my supplies to the attic.

Sorin was there, admiring the painting of our botanical garden. "You see it differently now, don't you?"

I nodded, noticing a full-length mirror next to the drawing of Snow White.

"I thought it would help you with the self-portrait," he offered thoughtfully.

I looked at the wall with all the paintings he had done of me, then back to Snow White. "I am feeling narcissistic, you know." I thanked him for the mirror, and then we both stilled at the sound of a truck door slamming shut.

The doorbell rang, and Sorin walked me down the first set of stairs. As I continued down to the front door, he turned toward my bedroom and disappeared.

An older gentleman waited on my doorstep, a pickup truck behind him. We introduced ourselves, and I led him up to the attic. Together, we covered each painting in a blanket and then tied them all with twine; this would protect them all during transport. One by one, we carried the wrapped paintings to the truck. He took a check from his pocket and handed it to me, saying that James would call in the future if he needed anything. He told me the pizzeria's grand opening was in two nights, inviting me to join them for the celebration. I stood on the porch and watched as he pulled away.

I shut the door behind me and went to the kitchen. Sorin fluttered past me, removed a stool from the island, and sat down. "How are you feeling, Mia?" he asked after a moment.

"Why is that the question of the day?" I didn't explain what I meant. I opened and closed cupboards. "If you really want to know ... I am hungry!" I complained.

"That is all?" he continued questioning me.

I stopped and turned to him. "Is that a trick question?" I wondered, suspicious.

His face held some concern. "I was simply inquiring," he said quietly. I could taste bitterness mildly but didn't ask him about it.

"I can't decide what to eat ... nothing sounds good, and I am starving." I slammed the cupboard door shut and opened the next.

"I will empty your refrigerator and freezer whenever you wish," he said.

I was glad to not have to do it myself.

"What about some fruit or vegetables for now?" His tone was ominous.

I looked at him, smiling. "Now? ... Are you offering something later?"

Sorin fought a grin. "You seem to be adjusting well. No reason to put off another exchange of blood, if it sounds enticing to you."

It wasn't the consumption of blood that sounded enticing to me. The only physical contact Sorin allowed was during the moments of drinking one another's blood. If I wanted one, I would willingly seem eager for the other.

His head tilted to one side, and he looked disappointed.

I brought a hand to my hip. "Despite what you are seeing, I feel totally ready." I waited for him to respond.

His shoulders fell, and he straightened his head. "You misunderstood, Mia. That's just it ... I am seeing very little now. Your colors usually filling the air around you have drastically declined." Sorin's eyes lowered to the counter in front of him.

My hand fell from my hip. I was actually amazed he was so disappointed in the newest change in my body. I shrugged. "It was an unfair advantage. Surely you realize that."

He looked back up at me. "It was an advantage I will deeply miss, love." He frowned as my stomach growled.

"I feel so hungry," I quietly whined.

"Then eat," he pushed.

I finally nibbled on some baby carrots and half an apple. It ceased the hunger pains, but I didn't feel satisfied. My stomach ached, and I pressed my hands against it. I looked at Sorin, recalling the taste of his blood and licking my lips. My eyes lowered to his neck.

"Just ask, Mia." His voice silky and low. He knew what I wanted before I did.

Fidgeting in my seat, I whispered back, "Offer ... so I don't have to ask."

His hand lifted mine and kissed it before he exited the kitchen. "Join me upstairs, and maybe I can sate your hunger."

My head lightened as he spoke. I slid from my stool, pursuing him. Looking down at my arm, I saw all the bruises were now absent. Once in the bedroom, I shed some of my clothes and crawled into bed. Sorin stayed fully clothed and didn't light any candles, trying to keep the line between necessity and pleasure clear.

He climbed onto the bed next to me, lightly kissing my cheek. "Next time ... I will only participate if you ask."

I ignored the comment, grabbed a rose, and handed it to him. I lay on my back and closed my eyes, waiting for Sorin to guide my mouth open when he was ready. I sighed as he held the flower under my nose briefly. Unexpectedly, the rose touched my face, tracing it delicately. I shuddered as I felt every petal tease my skin. It then brushed my lips, and I sucked in a deep breath. Knowing I would be denied any affection, I kept my hands at my sides, eventually collecting a handful of bedding in each. My heart's usual thumping was now quiet, and I was able to hear Sorin's extremely slow breathing. He lifted an arm as the rose lowered to my chin. I opened my mouth, ready to taste him, twisting and waiting for the contact with his wrist again.

His lips covered mine, and blood filled my mouth. Shocked, I opened my eyes and swallowed. Prickling chased the blood down my throat, and I quietly cried out. Muffled by Sorin's kissing me, I reached for him, wanting it all to continue. He quickly caught both hands, holding them to the bed. Sorin's eyes were ablaze, even without the candlelight. I fought in frustration. He pulled away.

"You know the day will come that I will be as strong as you. It may be years from now, and you may need to be starving. But the day will come," I fumed, annoyed.

A smirk crept over his moistened ruby lips. He leaned close to my ear and purred. "The day will come soon that I no longer need to restrain you. Your hands will be free to do as they wish."

I struggled in vain. "Hypocrite," I accused before his mouth closed over mine again in a crimson kiss. With every kiss, the sense of needles faded more. Giving up fighting, I closed my eyes. His hands lightly covered each of my wrists. I felt sedated and blissful from the last soft kiss. I lay still after Sorin moved away; I was utterly content. I felt a desire, a hunger, stir inside me, and I smiled. "Just ask," I whispered.

"Mia … ?" he began.

"Yes," I quickly said.

"You did not let me ask … you may not consent." His voice made my head light.

"Yes … to it all," I breathed. "I don't think I could ever say no to you, whatever your request."

Sorin moved closer, his breath on the curve of my neck. "I only hope you forgive me later." His fangs pierced my neck but only momentarily.

"Easily forgiven," I teased. His mouth moved to my shoulder, planting another kiss. "Still forgiven," I sighed, feeling dizzy.

His finger pressed my lips still. "Right now, it is mostly your blood flowing through your body. You will never taste like this again." Another kiss, this time on my upper arm. "Human blood tastes different throughout the body as it circulates to the heart and then away." Sorin tasted the inside of my elbow next. "I am merely beginning to enjoy you, Mia."

His finger lifted, and I gasped as his words were understood. I lightly shook my head, but never said the word. I couldn't find the strength to say no. A part of me did not want to deny him anything. Taking his time, Sorin made his way down my body, lightly nibbling my right ankle. He kissed my left calf and then began a trail back up my body. Each time, the bite was soft and brief. By the time he lifted my camisole to expose my ribs, I could no longer take the sweet torture. As he pierced the skin over my lower rib, penetrating deeper than all the others, I finally found my voice. "No more," I whispered. I felt drained physically from my body's being in pain one minute and pleasure the next. My mind raced with thoughts involving my new life, my new future. I tried to open my eyes as Sorin stilled.

Leaning over me, his eyes were fixed a few inches above where he had just tasted me. His fingers moved the thin strap from my shoulder, causing me to whimper softly. "Just one more," he said against my lips, lightly brushing them with his. Sorin lowered the fabric, exposing more of my left breast. I instinctively arched toward him, inviting him to indulge one more time. I closed my eyes, unable to watch as he savored the flesh just above my heart.

After his deepest kiss ended, he offered me his wrist, cutting it open for me. "It will help you heal quicker."

My whole body ached. Incapable of even lifting my arms to hold his wrist to my mouth, I only obtained a minimal amount of his blood. The uncomfortable explosions ensued, and I rolled to my side till they ended. Worry floated around me, tickling my skin. "I'm fine," I whispered. I knew more distance from Sorin would help keep his feelings at bay.

I swung my legs over the edge of the bed as I sat up. I stared at the rose painted in front of me, refusing to look at myself. If I focused on them I could feel every kiss Sorin had delivered; there were over a dozen, all easily felt.

In the bathroom, I left the light off and closed the door shy of an inch or two. I undressed and started the shower. Enjoying the hot water raining down on me, I slowly washed, wondering what I really looked like out of the darkness. The lighting changed in the bathroom, and I could smell candles burning. The door creaked open, followed by Sorin returning to the bed. I washed my hair and began to cry softly. I was ready to be like him completely. The old Mia was quickly disappearing, and the new me was ready to start living. I started to wish the movies had been correct: that a single bite from Sorin and a few minutes of hell was all it would take. I shut off the shower and wrapped myself in a towel.

He had only lit the candles near the bedroom door, none near the mirror. His emotions engulfed me as soon as I entered the bedroom. Walking to my dresser, I kept my back to him. Dressing in a long-sleeved jersey and satin pajama bottoms, I avoided his reflection. His self-torture only bubbled within me more, and I couldn't take it anymore. I turned to him, and brilliant sapphire eyes full of worry looked at me.

"Just stop!" I said, irritated. "I am well ... I am all right."

He sat up, away from the wall. "I feel it, Mia ... you are upset. You are forlorn about what I did," he said quietly.

I walked to the foot of the bed. "I will only say this once, Sorin. You may feel what I do ... but you do not know what is behind those emotions." I looked down at myself, totally covered. "Whatever I look like underneath these clothes, I consented to. I didn't stop you ... I didn't want to stop you. I only think it may be too much for me to see right now. Whatever I am feeling has nothing to do with ... your kissing me the way you did." I walked to the doorway. "Never assume why I feel what I do." Turning, I went to the attic, knowing painting would improve my mood.

Sorin joined me shortly afterward, sitting to the side, silent and content, just watching me. I felt his eyes move over my body. "Why then?" he asked at last.

"Why what?" I said, knowing what he meant.

"If what I did ..." he paused. "Why the tears, *amore*?"

I stopped painting, my shoulders falling lightly. It was easy to tell him everything I felt. "I am done, Sorin. I'm done with who I was weeks ago. I want to start a new life." I looked around the room. "This is no longer my home. I have no desire to stay in this house or this town. Let's leave and start a life together, far away from here." I turned to Sorin. "I cried because ... I jumped off the cliff, and the fall has yet to end." I shrugged. "I am ready for what is to come."

Relief washed over his face, and I returned to painting. "Tears of impatience," he said softly.

Hours later, I had the background on each canvas and was trying to decide which one I wanted to finish first. Standing up, I stepped back, pleased with each one so far. I opened my mouth to announce my decision.

But Sorin spoke. "I will stay up here if you want."

Confusion over what he meant quickly ended when I heard a car door shut outside. I looked down at myself, self-conscious.

He wrapped his arms around me and kissed the top of my head. "The kisses are nothing but shadows now, go."

I rushed to the door as he stayed in the attic. I swung open the front door just as Jennifer was about to knock. I startled her, and she lightly gasped. I apologized and opened the door the rest of the way, inviting her in. The sun was setting, and a nice breeze followed her into the house. She handed me a plate of baked goods, and I thanked her. "I'm amazed you haven't been by sooner." I smiled, teasing her.

Her face went blank for just a minute. "I don't know why I haven't been by before now." Jennifer looked around at all the covered windows.

"My sleep schedule is totally backwards ... plus, I will be working for Leo again soon."

Frowning, she didn't seem to accept my explanation. "And the owner of the black SUV in your driveway?" Jennifer looked behind me to the kitchen, then to the top of the stairs.

I sighed. She clearly wasn't going to give up her questioning. "Yes, I have a guest, actually."

She looked surprised, though she must have already suspected the answer. "Mia, do you really think this is the best time to ..." Jennifer tried to find the right words.

Sorin appeared and walked to my side. Jennifer jumped at his sudden presence. He placed an arm around me protectively and held a hand out to Jennifer. Greeting her, he gently kissed the top of her hand. Any reservations she had proceeded to melt away. Her cheeks blushed, and she smiled softly. Jennifer's eyes became unfocused, and her head swayed a little. He continued to flatter her in a hypnotizing tone. I reached behind my back and pinched him to get him to stop. Sorin said it was a pleasure to see her again, having not seen her since the funeral.

Looking from him to me, her eyes seemed to clear. "So how do you know each other?" she asked. "Other than from the ..." Jennifer let her voice trail off, but I knew she was thinking about Sorin's catching me when I fainted the day of my parents' funeral.

I took a deep breath, not sure how to answer her question.

I looked at Sorin, bewildered, and he squeezed me gently. His voice low and seductive, he answered for me. "Mia has known me for years."

Jennifer's eyes glazed over again, and she echoed his answer. "Mia has known you for years."

He slowly nodded his head. "I am here to help Mia through this tragic time in her life, and I would never hurt her."

She mirrored his gesture, and her head swayed absentmindedly. "You would never hurt her," she whispered.

Sorin looked at me briefly. Remembering what he had said about being able to influence humans, I knew these were all things Jennifer wanted to hear. He was offering her peace, a chance for her to no longer worry about me. I nodded for him to continue. He kissed my temple and turned back to her. "Mia is going through many changes right now and has chosen to begin a new life. One that may take her far away from here. She truly loves you for the friend you were to her mother. But it is time for you to let her go." Sorin stepped forward and took her hand again, kissing it. "You never need to worry about Mia again, Jennifer ... I will take care of her from now on."

My heart lightly fluttered as he spoke. I quietly asked him to get the box of my mother's belongings I had set aside for Jennifer and Gina. I turned back to her as he excused himself.

Jennifer still looked a little dazed as she walked toward me. "Well, I understand now why we have not seen much of you lately." She watched Sorin slowly move up the stairs. "You were busy being rescued." She walked to the door and hugged me tightly, her eyes watering. "I can see and hear how he feels about you ... I won't worry about you anymore." For the first time in weeks, I heard relief in her voice as she offered a real smile. I opened the door for her after Sorin handed her the box, and said good-bye. As I closed it I felt my own relief, knowing she could let go of any responsibility she felt for me.

"It needed to be done," Sorin said, wrapping his arms around me. "I wish you could have seen the concern drift away from her."

The car outside started and left.

I agreed. "I think she has been so worried about me that she hasn't really healed herself."

He kissed me lightly and walked to the door. Before I could ask, he answered, "I will return shortly; go work on your paintings some more."

I wanted more information, but he quickly stepped out the door, closing it behind him.

Chapter 12

Suddenly alone, I climbed the stairs. Halfway up, I lifted a sleeve, wondering if my skin had healed. The palest circular gray shadows made a path down my arm. I went to my bedroom and undressed in front of the mirror. My whole body was evidence of Sorin's crimson kisses. As I touched my stomach it growled. Nothing sounded good to eat, so I didn't bother going to the kitchen. I quickly redressed and went to the attic, returning to my artwork.

Sorin did return shortly after I began painting. He entered the room and just started watching me.

I stopped after a few minutes. "Aren't you going to tell me?"

He lightly smiled at my question. "Tell you?" he said, trying to look confused.

"I thought there weren't going to be any more secrets. Where were you?" I pressed, mildly hurt.

Sorin thought for a moment. "Not a secret … a surprise. Actually, I was getting you a peace offering." His smile faded. "You may not be mad at me for what you look like under your clothes … but I am disappointed in myself, Mia."

I turned back to the self-portrait, looking at myself in the mirror and then at the painting. I shrugged. "The crimson kisses you showered my body with are light bruises now." I looked in the mirror again, and he stepped behind me. "I consented, Sorin; let it go."

He looked down at my reflection. "You know that is not completely true." His forehead showed a few lines. "You called me a hypocrite … and you're right … I am weak when it comes to you."

I halted and faced him. "You are weak when you want to be … I want to do more than what you are offering. I want you to be weak at other times, but you find the strength to draw a line pretty easily." I looked him over. "So where is this peace offering?" I asked, now annoyed.

His light smile returned. "It will be here in a few hours."

I scowled and turned away. "Yeah, another box for me to not open."

Sorin chuckled, and then the room returned to silence. I had most of Snow White's face done when the doorbell rang. I jumped up and started toward the door.

He gently caught my arm at the top of the steps. "It is a meal … but listen to your body, for what it craves."

I pulled away, confused. "Promise me: no more riddles." I rushed down the second set of stairs, and Sorin moved to the kitchen. I opened the door, anxious.

A young man holding a pizza box stood outside. He was only an inch or two taller than I. Dark-brown hair in disarray and deep-brown eyes. His shoulders were very broad, and he flashed a perfect smile. "Hello there," he said, trying to sound smooth.

I coughed, trying not to laugh. At least five years older than he, I had a flashback to high school flirting games. "I'm sorry … please step in." He did, and I closed the door. Smelling the tomato basil pizza, my stomach rumbled.

"For the pretty lady," he oozed, handing over the pizza.

"I'm going to put this in the other room and get your money. Just wait here." I left his side and walked to the kitchen.

"Actually, it is already paid for," he said loudly.

I stopped at the opposite side of the dining room, turning to look at him. "Paid for?" I asked and then faced the kitchen. Sorin stood near the sink, a smirk on his face.

"Yeah ... it's really weird, you know." I held a hand up for the young man to stay at the door after he took a step my direction.

"What's weird?" I yelled from the kitchen. I stormed toward Sorin, tossing the pizza on the island between us.

"My boss said it was paid for, and you're my last delivery of the night."

I walked up to Sorin. "Really?" I called out to the young man, my eyes accusing Sorin.

Sorin moved to the pizza, opening the box. "You are still hungry," he said, keeping his voice low. "I feel it. Does the pizza smell appealing to you?"

I leaned over it, inhaling deeply. My stomach did a somersault, and I slammed the lid down. "That is odd," I called out again to my visitor, motioning for Sorin to get rid of the pizza.

"Well not that part so much ... but you didn't order it for yourself, if I'm right. ... I've never heard of a pizza being sent from a secret admirer. And my boss said I didn't have to come back tonight. He's never done that before."

I frowned at Sorin. "I don't think I can do what you are suggesting," I hissed.

Leaning close, he whispered, "I am suggesting nothing, Mia. If you are truly hungry and your body is ready ... it will be instinct. Smell him and then embrace what follows." Sorin picked up the pizza and slipped it in the refrigerator, stopping the scent from filling up the room.

My visitor grew bolder. "So … I'm free for the night now, if you don't want to eat alone," he said loudly from the front door.

I shot Sorin an aggravated look before exiting the kitchen. I stopped a few feet away from the young guy, effortlessly hearing his heartbeat. He smelled of tomato sauce, and he just stood still as my eyes moved over him. To my surprise, my mouth began watering. I took a step closer. "So you are free for the rest of the night?" I asked quietly.

His whole posture changed, and his pulse doubled. "Uh … yeah … yes." He stumbled over his words.

A chill climbed my spine, and I stepped closer. "You are not expected anywhere … soon?" I pressed, looking into his eyes.

"No-o-o," he said, oddly shaking his head.

"So you could stay awhile?"

His eyes went vacant. "I can stay awhile," he said flatly.

My stomach fluttered and my mouth remoistened as I heard his heart beat faster. I stepped closer, licking my lips slowly. I took his hands and moved us to the steps behind him. Stumbling backward, he plopped onto the steps, eye level with me. He was mesmerized, vulnerable. He sat there blinking; his mind completely blank. I sucked in my bottom lip, excited. My eyes moved over him, stopping at his neck. Suddenly my teeth ached, and pain registered in my lip. I winced, lifting my fingers to my mouth. There was blood on my fingertips. I ran my tongue over my teeth, confirming that fangs were present.

I leaned over him, resting my hands on his shoulders. "You don't mind if I smell you … do you?" I purred, close to his cheek.

His head swayed, and I leaned lower, closer to his neck. Inhaling deeply, I quivered. Scents I had never experienced before tickled my nose.

I swallowed hard, trying to fight the thoughts filling my head. His skin was a breath away, pulsing below my mouth as I lightly shook. Any control I had left me.

"Can I taste you now?" I whispered.

"Taste," he echoed softly, lying back and resting his head on one of the steps.

My whole body screamed to continue. I kissed the curve of his neck, sampling it. A moment later, I tasted blood. Heavy and metallic, but sweet somehow. Over and over again, I swallowed, as my surroundings faded away. The metallic honey kept filling me. Time stopped, and there was only the blood. I closed my eyes, continuing. I heard Sorin say my name, but I ignored him. *More* was my only thought.

"Mia!" Sorin said, louder this time. I opened my eyes momentarily. "Stop!" he yelled, and I stood up instantly, gasping for air. I searched for Sorin. "Send him home, Mia," Sorin's voice came from the kitchen.

I looked back to the steps. The young man was crumpled and pale. I tasted his blood on my lips and quickly wiped my mouth, removing any lingering red fluid. I walked over to him, astonished at what I had just done. Seeing his blood on my sleeve made me rush to his neck. Wiping it clean, I shook him roughly. "Get up!" I ordered. He stirred. Grabbing both his arms, I easily lifted him from the steps. "Stay here." I hurried to the kitchen, past Sorin, and to the fridge. I opened the door, pulled out the pizza, and returned to the stairs.

The young man was still groggy, stumbling around my foyer. I shoved the box at him. "Take it," I said.

He slowly blinked, threatening to come out of his current fog. He took the box, and I lifted both hands to his face. Taking a deep breath, I forced myself to relax.

Cradling his cheeks, I spoke softly. "No one was home when you delivered the pizza, understand?" His head bobbed and then jerked straight. "You tried to deliver the pizza, but there was no answer. Repeat it," I said, caressing his face.

"There was no answer," he mumbled.

"Now drive home … eat something, and then go to bed for the night." I shoved him out the front door, quickly closing it once he stepped outside. Leaning against the door, I sighed and slid to the floor.

Sorin slowly walked into the foyer, but I didn't look up at him. "I could have killed him!" I said, distraught.

He held out a hand, and I reluctantly accepted it. Cupping my chin, he forced me to look at him. "There was never the possibility of that happening, Mia. I stayed nearby for that very reason."

His words only upset me further, and I backed away. "Did you see … did you watch me?" I asked, uncomfortable with the thought.

"No … I kept my distance." He lightly frowned. "The first time is always overwhelming. It gets easier each time … don't worry."

I started toward the stairs. "I cannot imagine a next time," I told him.

We both went to my bedroom. I replayed the scene in my mind, describing it out loud as I changed out of my blood-smeared shirt. "He was so sure of himself, so arrogant. But the moment I reciprocated interest … his heart started racing. He became nervous and awkward, and my mouth started watering …" I dropped my shirt to the floor and raised a hand to my mouth. "I pierced myself with my fangs." I put on a clean T-shirt and turned to face Sorin, who sat in bed. "After that, it was like I left my body. I smelled his skin, tasted it … then couldn't stop myself." I lit a few candles. "I didn't stop … even after you said my name." I stood at the foot of the bed. "I didn't want to stop at all, Sorin." He patted the bed next to him, but I chose to sit at the foot of the bed, facing him. I wasn't ready to be touched; I still felt uncomfortable.

"You will learn to stay in the moment, to listen to the heart and stop yourself before it slows. You only did what was truly desired and needed. It is always your choice, Mia. … This time it was wanted." He softly smiled. The taste of sweet blood still lingered in my mouth. "His blood tasted so different from yours. Is that normal?" I had yet to brush my teeth.

Sorin grinned, and his head tilted slightly. "Well, it has been many years since I was so young and inexperienced. I explained to you that the purer they are, the sweeter the blood." Understanding what Sorin's words meant, I blushed lightly. "Anytime you feel the need to quench your thirst, I will be willing to offer myself." His smile grew, and his eyes darkened briefly. "I must confess, the thought of you piercing my skin … excites me, *amore*."

I collapsed on the bed and stared at the dark ceiling. "What a twisted compliment," I said under my breath.

Silence fell, and my thoughts lingered on how easily I had manipulated the young man. I thought of Anya, finally understanding how easily it would be to play with humans. Sorin had helped me gain a sense of control in my life. For Anya, it was just about playing with her food; oddly, compassion came over me.

"I will not assume … it is sympathy you feel for the young man. He won't remember the encounter, Mia."

I moved my head on the bed, facing him. "I was actually thinking about Anya. In no way do I condone the behavior you say she practices. But after tonight, I understand why she does it. It was easy to get lost in the moment."

Sorin looked surprised at my words. "Anya is still new to this life; she may change her ways." He sounded hopeful. "If it comforts you any … you should not feel hungry for many days now."

I looked back up at the ceiling, wishing I felt tired. "I'm going to go paint some more." I looked over at Sorin before leaving the room. "And I think I'm done with everything in the fridge and freezer."

He nodded. "It will all be cleared by morning."

I needed little sleep now, and I stayed in the attic, easily painting into the morning.

* * * * *

After a long shower and a quick nap, I was back to painting. Sorin joined me in the attic, and we talked about our future plans. I assured him a change of scenery was still a desire of mine. He asked to take over the responsibility of the arrangements. Within a few weeks, he said he would have new accommodations lined up for us. I finished the painting of Snow White a little after dark.

"It is breathtaking, Mia," he said over my shoulder.

I stood and smiled down at it. "Thank you." Looking around the attic, I felt a little closed in. "Outside?" I asked, walking to the door.

Sorin followed me downstairs and out through the patio doors. I sat on the patio, and he continued to the open backyard. I closed my eyes, laying my head back. I tried to use all my senses instead of focusing on just one, as Sorin had taught me. Slowly, I began to enjoy it all at once. The breeze, the scent of my mother's roses, the crickets singing. Suddenly there was the sound of a screen door slamming, followed by giggling. I didn't open my eyes; I knew it was Scarlett.

She ran into my backyard and sweetly demanded that Sorin do his magic trick. They spoke in hushed tones, but I heard them effortlessly.

"Please ... please!" she begged.

He chuckled. "Just once."

She jumped up and down on the soft ground. I opened my eyes finally, just to watch him collect all the fireflies. I gasped, sitting up quickly. Scarlett looked like she was surrounded by a miniature sun. Sorin stopped abruptly in the middle of his trick, looking at me. He waited. I motioned to continue and started walking toward the pair. He advanced to Scarlett and opened his hands. Half the number of fireflies than the time before flew around them. The light around the little girl dimmed some, and I was amazed.

"I am sure he can do better ... right, Scarlett?"

She turned in my direction, smiling. "Yeah! Do it again ... please," she requested, jumping up and down. I couldn't take my eyes off her.

Sorin leaned near me, whispering softly, "What is this I feel?"

My eyes widened; she was even more colorful up close. Not just a light around her, but different shades of yellow floated around Scarlett. "I can see her," was all I could say. I wanted to reach out and touch the air around her. "Do the trick for Scarlett again." Movement began to my left, and the light increased around her. I quietly laughed, looking at Sorin as he opened his hands for her a second time. "It's beautiful," I said.

Scarlett chased after the now-free fireflies, joyous shrieks escaping her.

Sorin wrapped an arm around me. My eyes watered. "I finally see what you have seen this whole time." Sorin kissed my cheek.

Scarlett returned to her yard, eventually going back inside her house.

Disappointed, I sat on the ground and looked out into the trees. Sorin started toward the patio, chuckling. I turned around. "Where are you going? ... We just came outside."

Sorin stopped at the sliding doors. "You are free, Mia ... there are no walls or bars around you." I jumped up and joined him, confused. "Go get dressed, and we will tour the colors of the night."

I was so used to staying at home, the thought hadn't even occurred to me. I rushed past him, racing inside and up to my bedroom, where I dressed quickly.

Chapter 13

A short time later, Sorin was driving slowly around town, allowing me to view the people walking around.

I was content seeing the first few through the windows around me. But then I said, "Please park … I want to walk around town, see everyone up close." I offered a smile.

Wanting to please me, Sorin parked soon after that. He looked around and then up to the streetlights. "Just try to stay in the shadows with me. Do not follow anyone too close. No eye contact either." He paused. One of the many bodily changes after turning was that of our sight at night or in poor lighting. Similar to tapetum lucidum in animals, we now needed one-sixth of the light that we'd needed before to see in the dark. But as a result, our eyes gleamed when the light caught them. If seen, it would be met by a confused look or second glance. "Allow me to lead," Sorin finally finished.

I smiled at his nervousness. "I'll be okay."

We walked slowly, and every time Sorin and I crossed paths with someone, he would explain the colors I was seeing. Most were generally happy, some stressed, and a few just plain angry. Without difficulty, I overheard conversations and began focusing elsewhere, as I felt it was an intrusion.

A dark alley caught my eye, and I moved ahead of Sorin on the sidewalk. Trying to entice him someplace extra dark, I turned down the alley.

"Mia," he said, unhappy and fully aware of my intentions.

I continued, knowing he would follow. Only instead of catching up to me, he purposely walked slower. If I stopped, he stopped, refusing to indulge me in a single embrace or kiss.

"I told you ... a little longer, love." His body tensed, frustrated.

Annoyed, I hurried to the other end of the alley. When I reached the edge of the darkness, I waited for him. Smiling and watching as he walked toward me, I sighed at the sight, delighted Sorin was the one I would spend the rest of my life with. The closer he came, the more his own grin grew. I only saw him, our future before us. Just a few more paces, and he would be next to me. He stopped, his eyes dropping to my side. As I looked to see what had caught his attention, something touched my hand, causing me to flinch.

She looked around three years old, with messy blonde curls and aquamarine eyes. "Lola," she said quietly, continuing to hold my hand.

I knelt down, totally taken aback. "Your name is Lola?" I asked, smiling.

She nodded, and I looked over her. She wore polka-dot leggings, and cartoon-character slippers covered her feet. A stained oversized T-shirt hung oddly on her small body. The smell of greasy fast food tickled my nose, and I noticed dried ketchup on her cheek. I slowly grew appalled at her appearance. She stuck her thumb in her mouth.

"Where are your mommy and daddy?" I asked.

Lola shrugged and continued to suck on her thumb.

As I looked up, seeing a gas station, Sorin lifted my other arm. I turned to look at him. "Can you believe this?" I whispered.

He was looking in the direction of the gas station. His eyes squinted, concentrating on something.

"She says her name is Lola. ... Do you think she wandered away from her parents?"

Something held his attention, and I looked back down at the little girl holding my hand. I noticed an abrasion on her forehead, peeking out from under her hair. I brushed her curls away. "Are you hurt, Lola?"

She just looked at me blankly, remaining silent.

Movement caught my eye: a couple near the pay phone started arguing and looking around.

"I think your mommy and daddy are looking for you, sweetie."

The young woman wandered around the parking lot, calling, "Cindy!"

I leaned closer to Sorin. "They should be ashamed of themselves, losing their child like this."

He watched them searching the area and eventually spotting Lola.

"Why are they calling her Cindy?" I asked Sorin softly.

I looked at the little girl again. "Is your name Cindy?"

She shook her head no.

The couple rushed in our direction.

"Cindy!" the guy yelled. "Come here."

I looked down at her as her eyes widened. Her little fingers tightened around mine. I didn't understand what was going on. Sorin tried to pull me back from the little girl, but she held tight. Lola's colors changed around her. They had been a dreary dark gray, but a brilliant blue overcame her as the couple advanced.

The young woman grabbed Lola by the arm, yanking her from me. "Come on, dear," she said quickly, leading her away. A shade of green I had yet to see swirled around the couple.

"Thanks … she's always wandering off," the guy said, a few feet from us.

The couple smelled of beer and cigarettes. Something nagged at me. I watched them, disgusted that they could treat their own child that way. Suddenly it all made sense. "She doesn't belong to them," I hissed, starting after the two figures before me. I realized Sorin had been silent the whole time. He grabbed my arm, keeping me from advancing on them.

"She doesn't belong to you, Mia." We both heard the guy speak as they walked away.

"Are they watching us?"

Sorin pulled me close, kissing me—well, pressing his lips to mine. My whole body shook with anger. A minute later, the door to the convenient store chimed, and he eased away.

I tried to wiggle free, and for the first time, was almost successful. "I'm telling you, that little girl is not theirs, and I will not watch them leave with her."

He loosened his grip. "Mia, relax … you are right. The little girl is not their offspring."

I looked at him, confused about everything. He already knew. "You knew?" I broke free from Sorin, shoving him.

"The male is AB, and the female is A. … The little girl smells O positive."

I stood still. "You mean blood types?" I turned toward the gas station.

"Yes. I also overheard the woman on the phone." He backed away and leaned against the building behind him, crossing his arms.

"What did she say?" I walked closer to him.

"She said they were going to drive all night so they could have the package there by morning and expected full payment at that time." I fumed as he continued. "The car they are driving is from out of state, and I can see deceit all around them."

My hands balled into fists at my sides. "She is not leaving here with them."

Sorin fell silent, and I began to pace in front of him. "Well?" I demanded. "You realize she is in danger. ... I'm sure Lola's family is looking for her. What are we going to do?" I turned toward the gas station windows, making sure the couple hadn't yet left with Lola.

"They have to make another call for an address. You lure the little girl to you." He looked down the alley. "Get her out of sight quickly and do not be seen with her, if possible."

Some of my anger melted away. "We'll find her parents, Sorin, and protect her until then." I wrapped my arms around him as he kept his arms crossed. "It is the right this to do," I whispered.

Moving away, he shook his head, unhappy. "This is no longer your place, Mia. You should not insert yourself in human lives like this." His eyes drifted past me. "But you would do this without me if I refused to assist you. So helping you is my only option."

I stepped back a few feet. "This may not be your place ... but I am between two lives right now. Not only does a part of me scream to help her, but another part of me screams I finally have the power to do so." I pressed my lips together, trying to stop myself from saying aloud what I was thinking. I failed. "You injected yourself into a life-or-death human situation, Sorin. I am here because of it. You chose to change my life. ... I am choosing to change Lola's."

We stood in silence, watching the door. Finally, they emerged; the woman walked to the pay phone, and the guy turned in the opposite direction. Lola didn't know which one to follow. Eventually she chose the woman and shuffled after her. Once the phone conversation began, the little girl was ignored.

"Down the alley quickly, Mia," Sorin ordered in a low voice, then he walked toward the guy who stood off to the side, smoking.

Lola looked around, sucking her thumb. As her eyes turned in my direction, I waved her over. She froze, looking up at the woman next to her. Yelling at the person on the other end of the line soon followed. I frantically waved Lola over to me again. The colors around her lightened as she walked toward me. Once she was close enough to me, I whispered, "Run, Lola!" She did, and I scooped her up and headed down the alley. Little arms wrapped around my neck, and I knew I was doing the right thing.

I turned the corner onto the sidewalk as soon as it was possible. With the cement clear at that moment, I stayed close to the buildings and walked back to where Sorin had parked the car. Not long after, Sorin pulled up, and I climbed into the backseat, settling the small bundle in my arms onto my lap.

"What happened?" I asked, not sure what to think.

"I convinced the sorry excuse for a human that a policeman had arrived and seen the little girl. He believed he had only moments to leave a free man and to abandon the little one."

I looked down at Lola, holding her tight. "You just let the two go?" I asked, upset.

"Mia … other matters are more pressing than revenge at the moment."

I sat back, mute for the rest of the short drive to the house.

Once inside, I sat her four steps up on the stairs and finally relaxed some. "Your name is Lola, right?"

She nodded sweetly, sucking her thumb.

"How old are you, Lola?"

She continued sucking her thumb and looked at her other hand. Eventually she held up three tiny fingers.

"What is your mommy's name?" I asked softly.

She removed her thumb briefly. "Mommy," she said quietly.

Any hope of getting some useful information drained from me.

"Daddy's name?" I tried.

"Daddy," said the small voice.

I looked at Sorin. "She can't offer us anything. We will just have to search for any missing girls around her age."

Turning back to Lola, the well-lit foyer showed how filthy she really was. "I am giving her a bath. She needs new clothes." I remembered he had just thrown out the little bit of food I owned. "Food too. … You are going to the store and picking up clothes and food. I refuse to reunite her with her family malnourished and wearing … that."

Sorin's eyes moved from Lola to me. "Mia, I have never bought anything for a child." He started to shake his head. I stepped right up to him and made it clear there was no choice.

"I am sure you would prefer to get her clothes and food rather than bathe and entertain her here, correct?" He backed away to the door. I looked at Lola. She simply watched the two of us silently. "It's easy … I think. Her clothing size is her age, and pick out healthy food." I couldn't look at her in such a state a moment longer. "You will figure it out. I have confidence in you … just go. We will search the television and Internet as soon as you get back. By morning, we'll know who she belongs to."

I started toward Lola. Sorin caught my arm gently. He leaned near me, whispering, "Remember that is a teacup on those steps there … Something you are less of each day. Be careful with her." He let go of me, and then he left.

I was suddenly paranoid I would break her. She was so small and fragile looking. "Let's go upstairs and give you a bath." I unhurriedly followed behind her as she awkwardly climbed the stairs. In the bathroom, I gradually undressed her after starting the bathwater. I threw away all her clothes as I removed them. I wasn't surprised as I lifted her shirt that it hid bruises underneath it. Lola's upper arms held multiple black-and-blue marks. Anger swiftly filled me as I recalled the way the woman had grabbed her at the gas station. She also had an odd bruise on each shoulder that resembled a V crossing her chest. I touched it lightly, a green-and-yellow color. Older than the other marks on her skin.

"Ow!" she said flatly, looking down at herself.

I lifted her chin and looked into her sad eyes. "No more ouches. I promise." I stood and shut off the water. "Ready for a bath?"

She stepped closer to the tub. "Bubbles?" Lola asked softly.

"Bubbles?" I looked at her, amazed that she'd said something without being prompted. Searching the bathroom, I knew there wasn't any bubble bath. I poured a few capfuls of body wash into the water and swirled it around, making bubbles. It didn't produce the smile I was hoping for, but she climbed into the tub with little assistance. I carefully washed her hair and body, her small battered arms enraging me.

I pulled the curtain half closed and pointed to my dresser. "I will be right over there if you need me." I walked to my dresser, wanting to find the couple who had treated her so badly; I would cover them in black-and-blue marks. I shoved clothes around as the anger built, filling my body. Tears moistened my eyes. "Bubble … pop." I barely heard the words drift from the bathroom. I flung open my closet door, searching for something to put on Lola until Sorin brought back clothes for her. My body began to shake; I wanted to break something.

Sorin rushed into the room, and I stopped. "Did you already go to the store?" He hadn't been gone long enough, and his hands were empty. "Where is everything?" I asked.

"I was almost there … when pure hatred filled me. I cannot even think right now. Worried about …" He searched the room. "It is just the two of you here? … I was concerned." He crossed to me. "Mia, you have to let it go."

I pushed him away, even angrier now. I moved to the edge of the bed, out of Lola's vision. "You didn't see her, Sorin." I pointed to the bathroom, speaking low. "I want to destroy something, hurt the two who—"

He stepped closer, stopping me midsentence. "I know exactly how you feel." Sorin's hands moved to his head. "All I feel is hate swimming around me, filling me. Stop, Mia." His body was tense.

"Bubble … pop … pop," Lola's tiny voice said to herself.

My hands balled into tight fists again. "Stop?" I said harshly. "As if I can just shut these feelings off. Maybe I am still a little human … because I can't simply shut them off or switch to happy." Lifting my palm over my chest, I added, "My heart aches for her. I want to make it all better, but I can't do it fast enough." I shook my head. "No child should ever be treated like that."

Sorin stepped toward me, and I backed away. "Mia, please let the anger go." His voice was softer and his hands were about to reach out for me. I held out a hand warning him to stay back. "We will find her family, Mia … we will right this wrong." He said it silken, taking another step to me.

I backed up again, my arm still out between us. "Don't you dare touch me, Sorin. I have never been so infuriated. Do not think you can make me forget what she has been through. Torn from her family and almost sold. …" He stepped closer and I backed into the wall behind me. Tears filled my eyes, and Sorin moved against my hand. I lifted my other hand, trying to push him away with both. "Just go," I whispered. Frustration now mixed with the anger already inside me.

"Please feel something else," he said. Both of my palms stayed at his chest as he softly pressed himself against me. His hands moved to each side of my waist. I turned my head away as a few tears fell down my cheek. Sorin lightly kissed my face then my neck. The anger flowing through me ultimately dissipated. It was impossible to cling to it as he kissed me. "Is not this much better, *mon amour*?" His voice was sultry.

My body lost its tension, and I sighed. "You didn't see her," I tried to argue.

"*Shhh* … we will do what we can. She will be back with her family soon." He kissed my shoulder.

"Bubble … pop."

I moved him away. "Just go."

I went to the tub and drained the water. I held out a towel and wrapped Lola in it, crossing it under her arms so I could comb her long blonde curls. I lifted a comb and noticed my toothbrush next to it. "Sorin … you still here?" He walked to the doorway. I stood facing him, beginning to untangle Lola's hair. "Don't forget a small toothbrush for her too." His eyes left my face and looked over the small child facing him. My body tensed up as Sorin now filled with all the emotions he had only moments ago freed me of. "I tried to tell you," I said quietly.

He moved slowly from the door, and I looked back down to her hair. The silence was short. We both jumped at a sudden crashing sound. Lola backed into me. The sound of plaster pinging down the wall disclosed what he had done. I circled the small body in front of me. "You try to comb your hair, and I will be right back."

Her tiny fingers took the plastic instrument from me, and she nodded.

I heard the sound of plaster crumbling all over again as Sorin removed his fist from the wall. I stepped out of the bathroom doorway. "Stop breaking shi—" I turned toward Lola. "Stop breaking stuff," I said, not finishing the profanity. There was a hole in the wall a mere foot away from my painting. His eyes fell to my wrist, and he started to leave. "I meant the countertop and now the wall." Sorin glanced back before leaving the bedroom. "You know I did not mean me." He left, and I walked back to Lola.

After delicately untangling her hair, I put it in a thin ponytail. I put a Band-Aid over the abrasion on her forehead, and we walked to my dresser. She sat on the floor as I found the smallest T-shirt possible to cover her with. After a few cuts with the scissors and some knotting, it fit her. I looked at her and sighed. "You're rather quiet, Lola." Her water-colored eyes just stared back at me as her thumb filled her mouth. It gave me an idea. "You sit there," I said softly.

My opinion was she needed a distraction, and then maybe she wouldn't suck her thumb. I felt she looked a little old for that habit. I opened my closet door and searched the bottom for an old box of mine. After a few minutes, I found the item I had searched for and set it between the two of us. Lola leaned over it, curious. I smiled, knowing it might work. "I will open this box if you remove your thumb. ... Big girls don't suck their thumbs."

She looked back down to the box, and a smacking sound soon followed as she pulled her finger from her mouth. I knew it was a soothing technique and just needed to be replaced with something else. I opened the box and pulled out a blanket first. A very soft knitted pale-pink blanket that my grandmother had made just before she passed away. Lola reached out and touched it.

"It is really a soft, huh?" Lola nodded, and I passed it to her. "You take it." It fell over her lap.

I removed a silver piggy bank and put it at my side. Next were a few baby dresses and a toy rattle. Looking down at my childhood memorabilia, I knew there was no longer any point in keeping them. Turning back to the box, I smiled. "This is what I was looking for."

Lola's eyes widened, and she moved forward.

I pulled out a blue stuffed bear from when I was her age. Moving the box from in between us, I put the bear in her lap, on top of the blanket. "I know he doesn't look very happy, but he is really sweet." I tapped his blue-colored heart-shaped nose.

She quickly hugged him and played with a small blue curl of fur on his head. She yawned, and I looked over to the bed.

"It is really late now." I pulled a book from the box. "Would you like a story?"

She lightly smiled and bobbed her head eagerly. I chuckled and stood up with the book. She jumped up, the blanket in one hand and the teddy bear clutched in the other arm. I moved to my bed and sat the book on it. Lola quickly joined me, excited.

I held out a hand to her. "Just wait right here … I will be right back." I swiftly retrieved a small wooden stool my parents used to keep in front of my bathroom sink when I was little. I set it at the foot of the bed. "Can you climb up by yourself?" I took the bear and the blanket, setting them by a pillow for her. She awkwardly climbed the stool up to the bed and then pulled the bear to her.

I sat beside Lola and opened the book. "I will read you a story my mommy used to read to me." She lay back against the pillows. I fought back tears, remembering the many times I had heard this story. A few minutes later, the story was almost done. A loud rumble made me stop reading. "Wow!" I looked over at Lola's stomach. "Are you hungry?" She nodded a yes. I closed the book and moved from the bed. Walking to the stool, still too afraid to touch her, I held out a hand to assist her down. "Let's go see if there is anything in the kitchen to eat."

She followed me slowly down the stairs, holding on to each of the wooden rungs at her side. When we reached the kitchen, I didn't feel comfortable letting her sit on a stool so high from the ground. I decided to get over my fear of hurting her. "Come here, Lola," I motioned her closer, the bear dangling by his arm next to her. I carefully lifted her to the marble countertop. "Stay right here, okay?" She turned to the bear, twisting his fur.

I searched the cupboards, finding nothing. Every box needed milk or eggs to complete the food item. I had finished all the crackers. Pasta and sauce was an option. Thankfully a car door shut outside. Relieved, I shut the cupboard doors. "Sorin is back," I announced, pleased, returning to Lola.

The front door opened, and the sound of store bags filled the foyer. We both looked to the doorway, waiting. He entered the kitchen, each hand holding multiple bags.

"Is there anything you did not buy?" I asked.

He looked down at his purchases and shrugged. "I tried to get everything she may need."

I slid Lola closer to me, making room for all the bags. "I think you succeeded." I spread out all the items around the small child. Sorin had food and clothes in the first half of the bags. I showed Lola everything, but there was little response from her.

Sorin noticed the bear she held and scowled at it.

"What?" I asked, defensive.

"Is that a child's toy?" he asked in a lowered tone.

I lifted a hand to my hip. "Yes, it was mine. … Why?" I was confused.

"It looks mad."

I lifted it from Lola for a moment. "Grumpy," I corrected. "I liked him because of the rain cloud on his stomach." I passed the bear back to the tiny arms reaching for him. I started to empty more bags. "There was a bright-yellow bear with a sun on his stomach ... but even as a child, I enjoyed a storm over sunshine."

He stood watching me sort everything he had purchased. "Some things never change," he whispered.

The last two bags contained toys, crayons, and a few coloring books. The last item I removed was a container of bubbles. I set it on the counter, and Lola grabbed them. "Bubbles!" she said loudly.

Chuckling, I began removing tags from the pajamas for her to wear. "She really likes bubbles," I said out loud.

I made her a peanut butter sandwich and sliced up an apple to go along with it. She finished it all and drank a small glass of milk. I left her clothes and toys on the counter. Helping her down, I took the toothbrush, bubble gum toothpaste, and some pajamas for the night. "I'm going to tuck her into bed." We left the kitchen slowly, Sorin following. I turned in his direction. "Let me know when you find something."

His face held multiple emotions. "Of course I will," he replied.

I followed the curly blonde head upstairs, changing Lola's clothes carefully. Not wanting to bump any of her bruises, I let her dress herself when she could. I put on my own pajamas, feeling tired by the time I helped Lola into bed. She curled up against my pink blanket and held the bear tight.

"I'm going to stay up here with Lola and rest," I said quietly, lying down and facing the child.

"May pleasant dreams greet both of you," he sent back.

I looked across the bed at her and frowned. My heart ached at the thought of what she must have been through. Shadows now appeared under her eyes, and she fought going to sleep. I could only imagine the thoughts filling her mind. "We are going to find your mommy and daddy, Lola," I whispered to her, lightly touching her hand. "Go to sleep now … and sweet dreams." Eventually her eyes grew heavier, and her heart slowed slightly.

I left the bedroom light on and closed my eyes. On the verge of sleep many minutes later, a whimper kept me from finally dozing off. I blinked as a low whimper sounded again. I looked over at her. She moved in her sleep, her heart began beating faster. Fully awake now, I sat up and rubbed her back. "*Shhh …*" I didn't know what to do. Her cries only increased.

"Mama …" she mumbled.

"Lola," I softly tried to wake her.

She stirred and opened her eyes. Looking around only distressed her more. Tears filled her eyes, and she tightened her arms around the bear.

"*Shhh …* I know, sweetie, you miss your parents. I know what that is like." I had no idea what to say that would soothe her. I patted her back some more, looking around the room, anxious.

Sorin must have heard everything downstairs. "Show her your roses, Mia." I barely heard him over Lola's crying.

I moved from the bed and lit all the candles in the room. She quieted as I shut off the bedroom light. Her heart began to beat even faster. "Now watch." I untied the curtains on the side next to her first, then on my side. I crawled back into bed and moved her next to me. "Look up there." I pointed to the ceiling above us. We both lay on our backs, my arm around her gently. "See the flowers dancing?" She looked up and rubbed her eyes. I pulled a tissue from the drawer next to me. Dabbing her eyes dry, I tried to calm her some more. "I will stay here with you if it will keep the bad dreams away." She cuddled against me, the bear still held tightly. She watched the ceiling with me, and her crying turned to a random sniffle after a while. I felt Lola relax and her eyes closed. Turning to my side I kissed her head. "It will be all better soon." She smelled so clean. The scent of my shampoo covered her. My thoughts drifted to how filthy and neglected she had been. Now bathed and in clean pajamas, she looked like a different child.

"Have you found anything yet?" I whispered.

"Nothing," Sorin said sadly.

I watched Lola gradually drift back to sleep. How was somebody not missing her? She let out a soft whine and moved closer to me. I wrapped an arm around her and then fell asleep myself.

Chapter 14

A couple of hours later, I awoke and carefully moved from the bed. I hurried downstairs to find Sorin. As I reached the bottom of the steps, I saw that the main room was empty. I realized there was only an hour of darkness left, so Sorin was probably outside. Not wanting to leave Lola for too long, I rushed outside. He sat in the middle of the yard.

"Still nothing?" I asked as he stood and turned in my direction.

"I searched the television all night," he offered, walking toward me.

"I don't understand … I don't think she has been missing longer than a day or two."

He took my hand and kissed it lightly, leading me back inside. "We will find her parents, Mia."

Passing the marble countertop full of pink and floral-patterned dresses and outfits, I picked out something for Lola to wear when she woke up. "I am going to take this upstairs. She shouldn't wake up alone in a strange place."

Sorin nodded.

I showed Sorin how to type any question into the little box on the computer screen, and then I headed upstairs. Entering my room, I set the little sundress with the fuchsia and lemon-colored flowers at the foot of the bed. I watched Lola sleep, so small in the middle of the mattress with all the blankets covering her. Climbing back into bed, I gathered her in my arms, holding her close to me. Lola's heart started beating faster. *"Shhh …"* I soothed, patting her back and tucking the blue bear between us.

For hours, I just lay there with her in my arms. How could her parents not be searching for her? The thought of never being a mother felt different now. Looking down at this helpless child who was currently dependent on me for her survival easily overwhelmed me. Lola's little hand moved across my neck, playing with a few locks of my hair. I swallowed hard, missing my parents and wondering what they would have said about my current life.

I could hear Sorin clicking constantly on the computer downstairs. As I stared at the roses dancing on the ceiling, the feeling of hunger moved around inside me. It had been a few nights since Sorin had consumed blood. The image of him feeding on the couple who had taken Lola filled my mind's eye, and the anger I'd felt the night before began to rise up in me. I closed my eyes and continued the fantasy. Blood pouring from the guy's neck as Sorin held him by the upper arms, causing well-deserved bruises. I watched it all play out in my head, envisioning the dark alley near the gas station.

"Mia!" Sorin's voice louder than normal traveled upstairs, bringing me back.

"Leave me alone," I said harshly.

Lola stirred, and I winced, regretting that I'd let him bother me.

Her aqua eyes slowly blinked open.

"It's still early, sweetie. ... Go back to sleep."

She sat up and looked around her. Her stomach rumbled, and I shuddered. I now understood why Sorin had complained about it.

"Let's go feed you," I said.

She went right to the stool at the foot of the bed and climbed down. I smiled as the teddy bear hit every step on the way downstairs. I slowly lifted her to the marble countertop again. As I poured milk into her cereal, she reached for the bottle of bubbles. "After breakfast," I promised, placing the bowl in front of her.

Putting the bubbles behind her and out of view, I piled all the clothes together, folding them neatly. I opened the package with the doll Sorin had bought for her and stacked the crayons on top of the coloring books. I sliced a few strawberries for Lola, glad the smell of food was no longer bothering me.

"How is breakfast?" Sorin asked as he walked in.

"She was pretty hungry." I took the empty cereal bowl and spoon, placing a small plate of cut berries in front of Lola. I put the dirty dishes in the sink. "I don't think she's the only one who's hungry. ... Are you going to step out tonight?" I sat on a stool next to Lola.

He watched quietly while she ate. "I think it best," he said softly.

I shrugged in response. "Don't be gone too long."

He left the kitchen, and Lola finished breakfast a few minutes later.

"Let's go brush your teeth and get dressed, sweetie."

I lifted her down, setting her feet on the kitchen floor and gathering her things from the counter. The still-gray cloud around her saddened me. I followed her to the stairs, passing Sorin at the computer.

Lola and I went upstairs. In my bathroom, we both brushed our teeth. I combed and fastened her hair into two curly ponytails.

Trying to cheer her up, I asked, "You want to put on a new dress?" She softly smiled as I lifted it from the bed. "You can wear it outside while we ... blow bubbles."

Finally her eyes lit up. "Bubbles!" she repeated. I helped her into the sundress, adding a light sweater to cover her bruises. After I changed out of my pajamas and into jeans and a dark-teal tank, we started downstairs.

"You are going outside?" Sorin asked as we passed him.

"Everyone's probably off to work for the day, and we're just going to the backyard."

He turned away from the computer screen. "That is not what I meant."

I thought I'd watched my last sunset nights ago, but the sun had yet to bother me. "I will be fine. … Teacups need fresh air and sunlight." Lola was impatiently waiting, her body starting to wiggle as she stood. I chuckled. "She really wants to play with some bubbles."

I followed her to the kitchen and handed her the bottle. Outside, I sat on the patio steps and blew half of the bottle, bubbles filling the air. A light yellow began to surround her, but she was still bathed in gray. We were outside a little over an hour when my arms began to tingle. I rubbed them at first, thinking it was goose bumps; I was feeling chilled.

The bubbles filled the backyard, and Lola chased after them. A breeze began, and the sun came out from behind a cluster of clouds. I heard Sorin calling me inside. Somewhat sad at the thought of his finding her parents, I ignored him.

"Bubbles!" the tiny voice cheered.

I continued watching her for another few minutes. My arms began to bother me more. I looked at them, and all seemed well. "Lo—" I stopped myself after the first syllable of her name. I looked around, but the neighborhood was quiet, not even the sound of wind chimes. I wondered if Sorin had anything to do with the noise being absent. I closed up the bottle, and she chased the last few as they floated away.

"Come on, Bubbles, let's go inside for a snack."

She looked at me, dismayed.

"We will go find something fun to do inside." Lola dragged her feet as she followed me. "Let's go, Bubbles," I said, reaching out for her small hand.

The exposed skin on my arms and face felt increasingly uncomfortable. As we walked inside, the sensation doubled, and I bit my lip, trying not to curse.

"Why don't we go get your snack?" I forced out, pointing toward the kitchen.

Sorin was getting a plate of food for the little blonde as we entered. I stopped, and he gave me a displeased look. "I will feed her. … You should go upstairs for a while." I stayed as he took Lola's hand. "It is a delayed response, Mia." His eyes fell on my arms and the rest of my exposed skin. "It will only get worse, and some distance will help."

He was right: my discomfort only intensified. "Sorry," I whispered as I walked upstairs to my room. I shut the bedroom door, overhearing Sorin tell Lola she could have a picnic with cartoons.

Sitting on the foot of the bed, I wanted to scream. It felt like sunburn, only my skin wasn't pink or hot to the touch. Lotion wouldn't help, and the thought of cold water hitting my body made me cringe. I soaked three washcloths in chilled water, wrung them out, and took them to bed with me. It hurt to move my arms too quickly. Lying down on the bed, I covered my exposed skin with two of the cold, damp cloths. The stairs creaked, and I waited, applying the third cloth. "You tried to call me in ... and I ignored you." I felt awful.

Sorin entered. "Why did you?" he asked.

I lay back as he sat on the edge of the bed near me. "I really wish lying was a possibility right now," I complained honestly. "I thought you found Lola's parents. ... I wanted a few more minutes with her." I looked away.

"Mia, we will locate her family," Sorin said gently.

"What if we don't find them?" I pressed my lips together, feeling guilty for wanting to enjoy Lola's company a little longer. "I mean, shouldn't you have found something if her family was looking for her?"

He laid his hand on my shoulder, where the tank covered my skin. "I am aware of the way you feel about Lola already. ... Maybe you should be more guarded in this situation. We could not possibly offer her a normal childhood. If we do not find her family within the next two days, we will consider our other options. None of which is a future with us, love."

I didn't want to talk about it anymore. "How long will the feeling of standing in a fire last?" I asked, changing the subject.

He looked at me with slight frustration. "Only you would deny the warning signs of impending pain. It should pass by the end of the day." He took the washcloths from my arms. "These will not ease the sensation. But if you promise to accept the sun won this battle and will avoid it after today ... I will make it end sooner." His lips turned upward in a slight smile.

I nodded, and Sorin paused, listening in on Lola before continuing. I repositioned myself, lying flat. Sorin's smiled deepened slightly as he looked down at me. "I do not think it is necessary to hold you down this time."

Considering most of my upper body was screaming in pain I agreed. "Please don't," I cringed.

He leaned over, lightly kissing me. "Don't force me to," he whispered against my lips.

Another light kiss relaxed me, and I closed my eyes. I felt it as he bit his wrist. "Ouch," I quietly fussed. He moved closer, and I licked my lips in anticipation. Sorin pressed his lips to mine, and I parted my lips. His blood quickly filled my mouth, and I swallowed, eager to lessen my extreme discomfort. Another mouthful, and some of the burning eased just a bit. A third time his lips met mine, but no blood was offered. As Sorin deeply kissed me, I whimpered, grabbing in frustration at the bedding beneath me. He was taking advantage of my current condition. I tried to turn away, but our lips stayed joined. He suddenly stilled as we both heard a light little laugh. It was the most beautiful sound heard in days. My eyes watered as it tugged at my heart. Sorin kissed me one more time. Very slowly he brushed his lips over mine. I felt every subtle line of his lips as he did, chills climbing my spine. I gasped at the new sensation. My stomach tightened, and I lifted my head, wanting to experience more. Softly smiling, he moved away. Sorin lowered his lips to my neck and blew lightly. I shuddered and quickly reached up to keep him near. My fingers only brushed against his sweater, and then my bedroom door closed behind him.

I opened my eyes to an empty room and screamed, my lips pressed tight. "I have never known such intentional torture. ... How can you be so cruel?" I asked.

The creaking of the steps stopped, and a mixture of emotions began inside me as I heard his response. "I suppose it is easy to inflict sweet torment now … knowing in a few short days the pleasure felt will be its equal." The steps squeaked again as he finished his explanation.

I sucked in a breath, wondering what it would feel like.

I heard the clicking of the computer mouse, along with cartoon voices. Lola lightly laughed again, and she became my only thought. All the moments I had already spent with her. Wondering how much longer she would be in my life. I stared at the ceiling, mulling over how long I should stay in bed. My skin still felt aflame. I realized the pain I now felt from the sun did mean my old life was finally over. Knowing I had completely turned did comfort me some. Other than a random little laugh and Sorin searching the computer, silence filled the house. It reminded me of what I had forgotten to ask. "I don't hear wind chimes. Should I thank you for that?"

He cleared his throat. "Well … they were disturbing your sleep, Mia, *dolce amore*." His voice was light.

I began thinking of my paintings, going over each one in my mind to pass the time. A while later, I heard Sorin ask Lola if she was sleepy. The cartoons and computer fell silent. I bent my arms, and they were still a little tender. Speculating about where I would be in a couple of weeks helped me pass some more time. The sunburnt feeling became dull, and I eventually left my bedroom.

As I entered the foyer from the steps, Sorin spoke softly. "It could have felt so much worse, Mia. I guarantee it will if you try that again."

I was about to rebuff his comment when I turned the corner and saw the two of them. My chest instantly tightened. Sorin looked forward, flipping channels on the muted television as a small body slept curled up against him. The colors around her had improved during the time I'd spent upstairs. "Look at her," I whispered. The emotions only increased as I watched Lola.

"Mia, don't do this to yourself," he warned in a hushed tone.

But I couldn't stop how I felt.

Lola stirred, and her eyes fluttered open. Once she saw me, a small sound escaped her, and she began to rouse more.

Sorin leaned in close as she looked my direction. He whispered in her ear, "She's mine, little Lola. ... But I can share with you." Sorin helped her down, and she ran to me. As she wrapped her arms around one of my legs, I fought a lump in my throat. "Why don't you two go paint? I will be resting if you need me."

I nodded and walked Lola to the kitchen. I collected the coloring books and crayons from the counter. Never wanting to hear her stomach rumble again, I carried a juice box and pack of crackers also. Sorin followed us upstairs and then turned to the bedroom. Lola and I continued up to the attic. While I painted, she colored quietly, mumbling a color's name every once in a while. Numerous times, I caught myself neglecting my painting to watch her. I finished the painting of Rapunzel brushing her hair. Looking at Lola's blonde curls, I decided to start Briar Rose asleep in her bed.

Hours passed quickly, and after a snack, I moved an empty canvas to her lap. It was small, and I lightly rested it over her legs. "What is your favorite color?" I asked her. She looked at the pile of paints between us, and I wondered if she would speak. Lola reached out and picked up a tube of purple. "Purple?" I asked.

"Purple," she echoed softly. Then she looked back and lifted up a teal.

"And blue?" I smiled.

"Blue," she said, a little louder this time.

Her eyes drifted back to the pile, and I laughed. "What else?" She picked up a bright yellow. "Beautiful colors, Lola." She smiled more than she ever had before. I squeezed a line of each color onto the canvas and handed her a paintbrush. The dusty yellow filling the air around her brightened as she painted, and the gray faded some. When she was done, I set the canvas against the wall.

"Lunchtime," I announced, turning back from the painting to face her.

She hopped up from the floor and started to the door.

"Wait up!" I laughed at how comfortable she was getting. But then imagining how the previous couple had treated her made my mood darken.

We went to the kitchen, and I fed her. As she finished her glass of milk Lola looked to the hallway leading outside. "Bubbles?"

I winced at the mere thought of going outside in the sun. "No bubbles right now, sweetie. Sorry ... maybe tonight." I felt bad to see how disappointed she looked.

"I can solve this dilemma," Sorin announced as he entered the kitchen.

We both looked over at him. I put the dirty dishes in the sink. He sat on a stool near the small girl. His eyes widened a little as he leaned close to her. "Bubble ... bath," he said, flashing a big grin. Scooping her up from the marble countertop, he set her on the floor. Every interaction between the two sweetly killed me a little. He would have adored and spoiled his own child. "Mia," he softly warned, feeling what I did.

Passing him, I took Lola's hand. "A bubble bath it is." I weakly smiled down at her.

She bounced up and down, excited. I let her play in the tub while I washed a few paint spots from her dress in the bathroom sink. After I finished hanging it to dry and picking out a new outfit for her, I joined her in the bathroom. Sitting on the floor next to the tub, I watched her play. She mumbled words every few minutes.

"Lola … do you have a sister?" I wondered if she had any other information that could help us in our search for her family.

She looked at me and shook her head no.

"Do you have a brother?" I asked.

Again she shook her head.

"Just mommy and daddy live with you?"

She saddened at the mention of them.

"We will find them, sweetie." I didn't know what else to ask. "What do your mommy and daddy's friends call them?" I had to try.

Looking at me she seemed to think about it. Lola puckered her lips and moved them like a fish.

"Are you a fish?" I laughed.

"Dada call me litta fish," she chimed.

I sat up at the complete sentence. It was slightly difficult to understand. "Daddy calls you his little fish?" I asked.

"Litta fish," she said, puckering her lips again. Playing with the bubbles, Lola was quiet.

I sighed and let her entertain herself until her fingers wrinkled. Then I got her out of the tub and dried her off. A short sleeved T-shirt covered most of her bruises, and a cute pair of shorts completed her outfit. I made two small braids in her blonde hair, keeping it from her face. Sorin was back to clicking on the computer. "Now what should we do?" I shrugged at her. She pulled on my hand, and we left the room. At the end of the hallway, she pointed to the attic stairs. "Do you want to go color some more?" I suggested. Lola started up the steps. "We'll be in the attic," I said to Sorin.

Another few hours passed as we painted and colored together.

"Up," the little girl sweetly requested, raising her arms to me. A light piercing of my heart followed. I couldn't imagine saying no to her. My eyes moistened with a few tears as I leaned over, carefully picking her up. Lola rested her head on my shoulder, wrapping her arms around my neck. I carried her slowly downstairs to my bedroom, laying her on the bed. She yawned and cuddled into the pillows. Staring up at the ceiling, she turned to look back at me. I lit the candles and untied the canopy of rose fabric around her. We both watched the shadows move above us. Drifting off to sleep, she curled into my arm.

As I undid the braids and played with the tiny curls around her face, I wondered if I was meant to be a mother after all. To feel so strongly about this child next to me after only a day was so foreign. Lola wasn't even mine, yet I felt so protective of her. I had already made my choice, and it ended the possibility of my bearing a child. I envisioned myself pregnant. Feeling a small life slowly grow within you must be even more intense. A part of me began to hope Sorin didn't find her parents for a few more days. Lola's heartbeat began to flutter faster, and a whine escaped her. I rubbed her back and kissed her forehead.

Sorin entered the doorway, and I turned my head his direction. "Did you find anything?" I asked.

Crossing his arms, he moved to the side of the bed. "I have found nothing." Lines appeared on his forehead. "It will be storming before the hour ends. If it gets dark enough, I will leave before nightfall."

I gently moved from Lola and sat up. "Why are you not waiting until tonight?" I could tell his hunger was not beyond putting off.

Sorin's eyes drifted between me and the small girl. "This is only complicating the situation." His eyes turned a deep blue as the candles caught them.

"Don't worry ... I'm fine, really."

His finger tapped at as lips as the lie left my mouth. He shook his head. "If we do not locate her family by morning ... I will turn her over to the appropriate authorities to find a more ... suitable living environment. You know she is not part of our future, don't you, love?"

My heart hurt as he spoke. "Deep down I do hope we find her family, Sorin. No child should be taken from her parents like this." I looked down at Lola. "But I cannot help any feelings that I may have developed for her."

He kissed the top of my head and left the room. Almost an hour of channel surfing and a few sounds of frustration from downstairs was the only thing that broke the silent air inside the house. As it began to storm outside, Sorin left.

Shortly afterward, the thunder awoke Lola. In a small voice she softly rambled about it raining popcorn.

I laughed. "If that was your dream I am jealous."

She climbed down the stool and started out the door as I put out the candles in the room.

"Wait for me, Bubbles," I called.

She stopped in the hallway, waiting until I joined her.

"Hungry?"

She smiled and said a soft yes.

After supper, the storm began to move past us. I handed her the few toys Sorin had bought the day before. Lola played with them on the kitchen floor as I washed the dishes and counter. Sunlight slowly increased at the top of the windows. I knew Sorin would not be back until dark, which was a few short hours away. We moved to the front room, and Lola watched cartoons as I drew many portraits of her in my sketchbook.

Another small snack, and then we painted again until dusk. I heard Scarlett squealing outside, and decided the little girl next to me had been inside long enough. "Do you like fireflies?" I asked, putting my paints away. "Do you want to go outside and play?" I said, after a few minutes of silence.

She smiled. "Outside," a small voice repeated happily.

"Let's go!" I cheered.

The sun was down enough that I knew it wouldn't bother me. Scarlett saw us enter the yard and ran over. The two girls looked at each other shyly at first. "Scarlett, this is Bubbles. ... Can you show her how to catch fireflies?"

In a few minutes, both little girls were laughing and running around. Eventually the color around Lola began to match the other child's. I cried a little as mixed emotions filled me, so distracted by watching the two girls playing that I had no idea Sorin had returned.

Scarlett's face lit up suddenly, and she darted in my direction. He kissed my cheek swiftly and rushed to the yard. The little strawberry blonde grabbed his hand. "Please do your magic trick … please." She bounced around him. The colors changed around the two little girls. Yellows faded to pinks and peaches.

Unable to watch what I knew would follow, I stood and went inside. Moments later, I could hear both girls squealing and begging Sorin to do his magic trick again. I stepped into my shower, trying to drown it all out. The water on my skin did distract me some. A strong sense of serenity moved inside me, and my heart ached as I felt his emotions. He was right: we both were slowly crossing a line. It was unfair to all of us if Sorin and I continued this. The girls were still playing as my shower ended. I dressed and went to the attic to paint. Putting in ear buds, I raised the music beyond what was now needed. I finished the highlights in Briar Rose's hair, and the scent of sandalwood slowly deepened. I looked to the doorway, and Sorin mouthed that Lola was asleep for the night. I turned away and moved a new painting before me. The mermaid would be next. Eventually the scent of sandalwood faded, and I knew he had left.

Looking at the canvas with purple, teal, and yellow spread across it erratically, I grew still, putting everything away and ending the music filling my ears. At the bottom of the attic stairs, I heard the television channels changing. Lola's heart fluttered as she slept in my bed. I turned to my room, wanting to be near the small child in it. She slept with her arms around the blue teddy bear. Climbing into bed, I curled around her little body. A random laugh escaped her. I closed my eyes, enjoying the smell of her, the sound of her breathing. The clicking of the television channels changing stopped. I opened my eyes, nervous. An overpowering feeling of relief and disappointment washed over me. I sat up as Sorin raised the volume just enough for him to hear it. I kissed Lola's cheek, not wanting to leave her side.

He called my name softly a few minutes later. As I walked down the hallway, he stepped to the foot of the stairs. "You found her parents," I said flatly.

He motioned for me to join him, but I stayed.

"Yes … we know where Lola belongs now." He sounded a little torn himself.

My eyes watered, and frustration built. "They just realized she was missing? … Why haven't they been looking for her?" I began to cry.

Sorin slowly ascended the stairs. "They couldn't, Mia. Lola's family was in a car accident. Many nights ago, they were headed home from a vacation away from their home state. They think Lola's dad fell asleep behind the wheel." Halfway up the steps he paused. "They rolled down an embankment and were not found until today. Both her parents are in critical condition and still unconscious. Neither was able to ask about their daughter, Mia. No identification was found in the rental car. All of Lola's belongings were absent, along with her car seat. The police did not know a child was missing."

Visions of the bruise across her chest filled my sight. "She has an older bruise in the shape of a V from her shoulders to her chest," my voice cracked. "It must be from her car-seat straps."

He continued upstairs, moving closer to me. "The young couple at the gas station must have seen the accident."

I backed to the wall behind me. "So they robbed the parents and kidnapped Lola," I whispered, disgusted.

He nodded, now a few feet from me. "It just took the police a while to trace the rental car and contact Lola's relatives." Sorin smoothed my hair and wrapped his arms around me.

"Now what do we do?" I asked, heartbroken.

He squeezed me lightly. "We get little Lola Fischler to her family. She has many relatives waiting for her return."

I pushed him away. "Fischler?" I repeated. The tears flowed. "She told me her dad called her his little fish. ... I didn't know it was her name."

He put his arms around me, trying to comfort me. "*Shhh* ... you had no way of knowing what that meant."

I shook my head and forced him away again. "Just take her," I said, my voice rising. Turning to flee back to the attic, I held out a hand to not follow. "She has been missing for days now. Her family must be sick with worry ... wondering if they will ever see her again." I roughly wiped at the tears falling. "If you take her now, she can be with her family before morning." I hurried up the stairs. "Just go," I said bittersweetly.

Returning to music screaming in my ears and another painting to start, I waited for it to be over. I was painting some shells on the beach the moment Sorin departed with Lola. I stared at her painting, knowing she would be back with her family soon. Convincing myself I'd known this would be the outcome all along, I focused on how happy she would be shortly. Gradually all the sorrow turned to contentment. Lola was going back where she belonged.

Chapter 15

Another hour passed, and I finally ended the music. I was calm now. I stopped painting, came down from the attic, and walked around the silent house.

Sorin had left a brief note for me in the kitchen. He was going to drive to a police station a few towns away, so they could not possibly trace Lola back to us. I crumpled up the note and threw it away, along with all the food and a few abandoned toys on the kitchen floor. I was walking to the front room when a car door shut outside.

Sorin opened the front door, weakly smiling at me. "Lola will be with her family soon, love."

My shoulders fell, and I still felt melancholy. I crossed to him, letting him comfort me.

"We did a wonderful thing, Mia," he offered gently.

"I know." I shrugged.

We walked outside, staying there until the sun threatened its presence. Once back inside, I began telling him how much I had painted. I wanted him to come up to the attic to give his opinion.

He started to follow me toward the stairs, but then he turned to the sofa at the last minute. *"Un attimo il mio amore."* Picking up the remote control, he turned on the television and stood in front of it. I waited in the foyer as silence filled the air. After a couple of clicks, Sorin grinned and turned to me. "Come see," he said pleasantly.

I walked to his side and faced the television. A crowd of people and reporters stood outside a police station in another state. A man in uniform was releasing a statement. In the background, a tall blonde with similar features to Lola's held her on her hip. Words moved across the bottom of the screen. It explained that the child had been found the night before. Lola's mother had awoken just an hour before, and the doctors were hopeful her father, too, would regain consciousness and survive his injuries. With each word moving across the screen, I felt better. I stepped closer to look at the little girl with the curly blonde hair. She held a blue bear by the arm. I lightly laughed, touching it on the TV screen.

"She refused to let that thing go," Sorin said, smiling.

I turned back, throwing my arms around his neck. "She looks so happy," I said, resting my head on his shoulder.

"Very happy," he agreed, turning off the television.

We went up to the attic, and I showed him the paintings I had finished. My stomach stirred a little, and I placed a hand over it. The thought of feeding on some stranger still turned my stomach.

Sorin leaned over my shoulder and whispered seductively, "All you have to do is ask." His hands moved over me, pulling me back against him. "Or we could wait a few more days," he teased softly.

Without even realizing what I had done, I spun around and knocked him to the floor. I was now lying on top of him. A surprised look covered his face, and I was equally shocked. He laughed, cupping my chin.

"I don't think my bones are in danger any longer." I pressed myself against him and lowered my face for a kiss.

Sorin's eyes sparkled as I looked down at him, lingering on mine just before our lips met. "No ... I think I may be the one in danger." He grinned.

I kissed him quickly, chills climbing my back. His other hand began touching my neck. I found both his hands swiftly and pinned them to the floor above his head. Kissing him more deeply, I sought his fangs to pierce my tongue with.

Sorin turned away. "Wait, Mia," he forced out quickly.

"No," I said, determined.

His neck was completely exposed to me, and I began kissing it. He shook beneath me and started to struggle. "I am only concerned for our current surroundings, love." I stopped, lifting my lips from his neck. He looked around the room, and then I did.

Not understanding what he meant, I said, "Sorin … I promise you I do not need music and flowers." I began kissing him again. My mouth watered as I tasted his neck.

He twisted his hands free and intertwined our fingers. Turning his face back to me, he forced me to desert his neck. Sorin spoke quickly before I could kiss him. "There is a box waiting for you to open it."

I grew still. I had completely forgotten about the box from Monique. "It can wait," I said slowly, trying to convince myself. My hesitation was an opportunity for him to sway me further.

His liquid voice began. "I opened the box … I have seen what was sent."

My head began to cloud. I stood up, freeing him. "You opened my gift?" I asked confused.

Sorin stood, taking my hand sweetly. "I know Monique … and I knew this moment was close. So I wanted to make sure the contents were worthy of you."

Even more confused, I allowed him to lead me downstairs. He stopped me just outside the guest room door. "It is sitting on the bed." He fought a smile and continued down the hall to my bedroom.

I entered the guest room and turned on the light. The brown box sat at the foot of the bed, unsealed but closed. I walked toward it and picked it up. Sorin moved around my bedroom, a blur passing the guest room door and then back. I moved the tissue paper inside the box, touching fabric. Thin satin straps became visible, and I let the box fall to the floor. I gasped at how beautiful it was. Walking to the side of the bed, I spread out the garment to admire it. It was a gown, sheer black with tiny black velvet bows randomly placed. The straps crossed over in back and the front fell to a deep plunge. I just stared at it in awe. Sorin cleared his throat, and I blinked.

"I'm sorry," I said awkwardly. "It is just so beautiful." I recalled the conversation he had with Monique. "Sorin, can you tell me something?" I asked quietly.

"I have no secrets," he replied.

"I could hear Monique asking you questions at the end of the conversation the two of you had." I paused. "I believe there were four of them. … What did she ask you?"

I slowly undressed, waiting for him to answer.

"You are correct, Mia. There were four questions."

I waited, anxious.

Sorin continued. "Monique asked me if I had finally found someone. Then she asked if the woman was present. The third thing she asked was if I had intentions of giving myself to you … making a permanent bond."

I slipped the gown over my head.

"If you recall, I answered yes to all three of those questions, love."

Passing the mirror near the door, I began to feel nervous.

"And the last question?" I pressed.

Sorin lightly laughed. "She asked what color I would like to see you in."

I walked to my room, candlelight spilling from it. Sorin waited in my bed, and I passed him to go to my dresser. I opened the bottle of oil he had sent for, putting a few drops on my skin. Turning around, I noticed the painting he had done of me was absent. Looking about the room more, I realized the nightstands were bare also. Sorin sat at the head of the bed, his back to the wall. No shirt, the satin sheet lifted to his waist. His eyes remained closed as I moved closer. My missing belongings no longer mattered.

"No music or flowers," he said, breaking the silence.

I moved to his side of the bed. "Not much of anything actually," I whispered, looking around the room and then down at what I wore, touching it softly.

"I will keep my eyes closed if you wish," he said sweetly, but my mouth watered, and the bitter taste quickly filled it. I made a displeased sound and reached out to shove him. Sorin caught my hand and pulled me to his lap. His eyes opened to reveal the deepest purple.

I bit my lip and smiled, thrilled that this moment had finally arrived. "As long as there is candlelight ... you are forgiven." I kissed him, moving my hands to his neck.

He pulled back, kissing my shoulder. "I was not about to miss the first time the colors filled your eyes." His voice caressed my skin.

I turned back to the mirror and saw what he meant. My eyes matched his. I blinked a few times, staring at myself until he kissed my shoulder a little too deeply. "Owww!" I yelped, surprised. I turned back to Sorin. I kissed him repeatedly, raking my tongue over his fangs and cutting myself. He moved me to my back, covering me with kisses through the thin fabric. His thumb brushed my lips, and I felt every ridge of his thumbprint, shivering at the sensation. I pushed him back, and he slammed against the wall with a thud.

Sorin tried not to smile as my eyes widened. "Should I fear being broken?" he said as he advanced on me again.

Grabbing him by the upper arm, I flipped him to the middle of the bed. A deep moan rumbled in his chest. He wore his thin ebony pajamas bottoms. My eyes roved over his body. I kissed his chest, tasting his skin. A few more kisses made a trail to his neck. I buried my face in it, savoring the taste of him. My mouth moistened, and my teeth ached briefly. Sorin's arms flexed under my hands, and my grip tightened. As my body began to tremble, I refrained just a moment longer.

"I think I owe you a few bruises, love," I purred near his ear. Sorin's whole body tensed below me, and I smiled before piercing his skin. I sighed as light fireworks filled my mouth. Light-headed, I pulled away, and my grip weakened around his arms.

Quickly his hands moved around me, bunching the thin fabric between us. "Forgive me," he forced out through his clenched teeth.

My eyes shot open, the word "no" not fully leaving my mouth, as the sheer fabric tore away from my body.

A few moments later, I didn't care about the destroyed gown, and by nightfall, I was pleased that Sorin had removed the items from my bedroom. He teased that it would be a while before I adjusted to my new strength. I kept my promise and tasted Sorin multiple times, leaving marks with each expression of affection. I could now feel each bite I made—as if I were bitten—but that did not make me stop. ...

* * * * *

Just a week later, my paintings were complete, and arrangements were made for us to begin traveling. I left a long letter for the mama bears, along with my last set of paintings for the coffee shop. Sorin promised they would be delivered after we left.

For the first and last time, I visited my parents' graves. I sat in the dark and spoke to each of them. Telling them how much had changed. Confessing how hopeful I was for spending the future as what I had finally become. Saying good-bye, I found closure; I was ready to move on from the life I was leaving.

As Sorin and I walked from the dark graveyard, our lives together began. He had become my reason to continue living, and I became his reason to start.